BLOOD RECKONING

A JOHN JORDAN MYSTERY
BOOK 29

MICHAEL LISTER

Blood Pathogen
Beneath a Blood-Red Sky
Out for Blood
What Child is This?
Blood Reckoning

(Burke and Blade Mystery Thrillers)
The Night Of
The Night in Question
All Night Long

(Jimmy Riley Novels)
The Girl Who Said Goodbye
The Girl in the Grave
The Girl at the End of the Long Dark Night
The Girl Who Cried Blood Tears
The Girl Who Blew Up the World

(Merrick McKnight / Reggie Summers Novels)
Thunder Beach
A Certain Retribution
Blood Oath
Blood Shot

(Remington James Novels)
Double Exposure
(includes intro by Michael Connelly)
Separation Anxiety
Blood Shot

(Sam Michaels / Daniel Davis Novels)
Burnt Offerings
Blood Oath
Cold Blood
Blood Shot

(Love Stories)
Carrie's Gift

(Short Story Collections)
North Florida Noir
Florida Heat Wave

Delta Blues
Another Quiet Night in Desperation

(The Meaning Series)
Meaning Every Moment
The Meaning of Life in Movies

Sign up for Michael's newsletter by clicking here or go to
www.MichaelLister.com and receive a free book.

For Sarah Burris
Librarian, artist, and human being extraordinaire!

JOHN JORDAN AUDIOBOOKS

MOST OF THE John Jordan mystery thrillers are available on audiobook — and all will be soon.

CLICK HERE for more information and audiobook samples.

SERIES SALE

For a limited time the entire John Jordan series is on sale!

CLICK HERE to complete your series for the best price EVER!

CHAPTER ONE

"HAVE YOU HEARD FROM CARLA?"

I immediately recognize the voice as that of Carla and John Paul's neighbor, Miss Minnie. She's a retired elementary school lunchroom lady who's too old and infirm to give John Paul the care he needs, and Carla only uses her when she doesn't want me to know what she's doing.

"Not today," I say. "Why?"

Anna's disapproval and disappointment are palpable. I can feel it even though I'm not looking at her. She had asked me not to answer my phone.

"She's running late to pick up John Paul," Minnie says.

"How late?" I ask.

Anna drops the pen she's holding onto the kitchen table, closes the notebook and file folder, and stands.

We had been working on a way to pay for Nash's college tuition and cover the girls' growing expenses, which was tense and unpleasant anyway. Me allowing the interruption provided a target for her to focus her frustration and irritation onto.

"Few hours. Said she'd be here by dark, and I need to—"

"Want me to come get him?" I ask.

Anna lets out a sigh and walks out of the kitchen.

"Could you? I hate to ask again, but . . ."

"I'm happy to," I say. "I'll be there in a few minutes."

CHAPTER
TWO

"CARLA IS RUNNING LATE to pick up John Paul, and Minnie asked if I could get him," I say.

"And of course you said *yes*," Anna says. "Doesn't matter what we're in the middle of or what we have planned."

After torturing ourselves with bills and budgets, we have a game night planned with the kids.

"We can still do everything," I say.

"No, we can't. And you don't care that we can't."

"You know that's not true. Of course I care. But I can't leave him with Minnie," I say.

"His mama does," she says.

"I wish she wouldn't."

"I *wish* you could see what you're doing," she says. "How it makes us feel. You drop everything anytime Carla needs you. She knows you will. She counts on it. She manipulates you and you enable her."

It's true that I try to take care of Carla and John Paul as best I can —especially John Paul, who needs far more than Carla can give him.

"I . . . I don't see it that way."

"How do you see it? Please tell me."

"I feel responsible for them."

"You feel responsible for everyone."

"That's not true and not fair."

She knows I've been working on my co-dependent tendencies to be overly responsible for others and my savior complex. She's using a vulnerability and weakness of mine against me.

"Sorry," she says. "I should've said that in a different way. You do so much for so many, but you can't do everything for everyone."

Even in the midst of dealing with challenges, disagreements, or actual arguments, I find Anna intensely alluring, irresistibly captivating, and incredibly attractive.

I take a moment and really look at her, study her for what seems the billionth time.

The fine lines on her face are like stanzas from a prose poem that tell a sacred story, and her brandy-brown eyes are deeper and hold more wisdom than even the day before. Her hair is just as thick as it ever was, and she keeps it brown and longish, at least in part because she knows how much I like it that way. And though she takes good care of herself and is vibrant and athletic and still remains stunning, she is aging, as am I, our lives having reached the tipping point where we're nearly guaranteed to have fewer days ahead than behind us.

"You don't feel responsible for John Paul?" I ask.

"We do so much for that child—more than anyone else. Including his own mother."

"We were going to do everything for him."

When Carla found out she was pregnant, she had asked Anna and I to adopt her baby when she had it, and we had agreed.

"Yeah, but she changed her mind about that, didn't she?"

"Don't hold that against John Paul."

"I don't. I'm not. That's not what this is."

"Are you sure?"

She takes a deep breath. "I'm gonna take a moment before responding to that."

Her anger has hit a new level.

"I just asked you a question," I say.

"No, what you did was imply that I'm punishing a child for his mother changing her mind about us adopting him."

"Think about all the things you've said to me," I say. "That I'm being manipulated. That I'm enabling bad behavior. That I feel responsible for everyone and put their needs before my family's. That I've ruined tonight by agreeing to go get John Paul. All I did was ask you a question."

"Not true," she says. "And you know it. You told me not to hold Carla's decision against John Paul, and when I said I don't you asked if I was sure."

"You're right," I say. "I didn't just ask a question, and I shouldn't have said that's all I did. I really don't want to argue about this. We can still do everything and—"

"How?" she says. "How can we do everything?"

"You could go with me to get him, and we could continue our budget conversation on the way, and we can still do game night when we get home—and let John Paul join in."

She shakes her head. "I don't want to waste our night arguing, but . . . you're not being . . . Your solution to paying for Nash to go to college and all the girls' expenses is we'll figure it out. We just do it and then figure it out. It's the same thing you're doing with John Paul. You say *yes*. Carla or Minnie or whoever asks, and you say *yes*. You always say yes. Then try to make it work."

"And doesn't it?" I ask.

"No. We've got too much debt and we're operating on a deficit. We're overloaded with our own kids and responsibilities, and you're saying yes to more—more debt, more responsibility, more energy and time we don't have. We're operating in a deficit as a couple and a family."

"We have to send Nash to college," I say. "We just have to. And John Paul is family."

"So we're gonna send him to college too?"

"Figured we would," I say. "When the time comes. We'll have plenty of money by then."

"We'll still be paying off Nash's and the girls' student loans."

"So we'll add his to it," I say.

She shakes her head, but the hint of a small smile begins to twitch on her lips.

"What else are we gonna do with our money?" I say.

"Retire," she says. "Travel. Not leave a mountain of debt for our kids."

"You're saying it's their debt anyway, but we won't."

"Of course we—"

"That's what life insurance is for."

"So your grand plan is say yes to everything and maintain good life insurance?"

I laugh.

A little of the tension dissipates.

"I don't say yes to everything," I say. "Just to the things the kids need. It's not like we're getting ourselves much of . . . anything. But I bet I can live on less than I am."

"I can't imagine how," she says. "You don't spend any money on yourself."

"I could sell the truck you got me and get a cheaper vehicle," I say.

"No. Absolutely not. That was a gift. But you know what would make a huge difference . . ."

I know what she's going to say. I pay my ex-wife, Susan, a lot of child support for Johanna each month even though Johanna lives with us and only visits her mom occasionally. It bothers Anna that money meant for Johanna is actually enabling Susan to live in the manner to which she is accustomed.

"It's obscene for us to be giving money to Susan each month when Johanna lives with us."

"And how long do you think she would live with us if I even brought up the subject with Susan? I'm not going to risk losing Johanna. I can't."

"I know."

"Then please don't bring it up again," I say. "Just see it as what I have to pay to have my daughter."

She nods. "Okay. I won't bring it up again."

"And I'd appreciate it if you could really let it go—not just not mention it but process it so it doesn't bother you anymore. You know you don't have to say anything for me to sense that you resent it."

She gives me a warm smile and nods again. "My sensitive, empathic husband. Yes, I'll work on letting it go."

"I can get a second job," I say.

"You don't have enough time as it is," she says. "Neither of us do. We can't work any more than we already are. Now . . . if you want to get a different job . . ."

I give her a quizzical look.

She says, "Have you forgotten what started this conversation?"

"I'm trying to block it out as we go."

"And I don't mean the drop-everything-every-time-Carla-calls conversation. I mean the original financial conversation."

"Nash's college."

"You hating your job and wanting to—"

"I don't hate it," I say. "I just miss Reggie and I . . . don't care for Fred Miller's . . . approach to being sheriff."

"So look for something else," she says. "Preferably something with better pay and less hours. Something you can be happy doing for the rest of your life. 'Cause neither of us will ever be able to stop working."

CHAPTER
THREE

IF I'M honest with myself, I don't just feel responsible for Carla. I feel guilty. And that guilt contributes to my level of care and commitment when it comes to both her and John Paul.

I used to spend almost all night every night with Carla—back when I was single and trying to get sober. Back before I eventually abandoned her for Anna and a happier life.

As a teenager, Carla worked the overnight shift at Rudy's, her dad's 24-hour diner in Pottersville, where I used to live. Since I didn't sleep much, I'd sit in the back booth and read, keeping an eye on the place while she slept in between waiting on customers.

Carla had been a deeply sad but equally strong motherless young woman raised by an absentee, alcoholic father. In many ways, I was all she had, and despite my best intentions and inconsistent efforts I had become just as absent as her father.

It had started when Anna and I had finally gotten together. It had been completed when we moved from Pottersville to Wewa. I told myself I would visit, that I would keep a close eye on her, that I wouldn't abandon her like everyone else had, but I had unwittingly done just that.

I can tell the guilt and other strong emotions I'm feeling are causing me to think of all this in extreme terms that lack proportion and nuance, but being aware of the fact doesn't mean I can do anything to change it.

"How worried are you about Carla?" Anna asks.

"I wish she'd answer so I know she's okay, but . . . I'm not overly worried yet."

In the end, Anna had decided to ride with me to pick up John Paul. We are in my truck on the Main Street of our little town, passing beneath a canopy of oak tree branches and fog-dimmed street lamps.

It's the second week of August during one of the hottest and wettest summers we've ever had. Of course, in this part of Florida every summer feels like the hottest and wettest, but the number of temperature and rainfall records set this summer means this year it doesn't just feel that way.

I am grateful to have her with me—not only because I always like being with her but also for her obvious effort toward reconnection.

Our discussion wasn't all that intense and our disagreements weren't extreme, but it's easy to let seemingly small ruptures build up overtime. Repairing them as quickly as possible is absolutely essential to re-establishing intimacy.

I never want us to waste the time we have arguing about how much more time together we wish we had, never want our disagreements to lead to unproductive arguments and building resentment.

I'm worried about Carla, but I'm trying not to jump to conclusions or obsess. I know all too well how many horrible things can happen to a vulnerable young woman, and ordinarily my mind would run to the possible threats and potential crimes she could fall victim to, but I'm trying to do better tending my thoughts and managing my mind.

At this point, I'm thinking this is more likely an act of irresponsibility than an indication of something wrong, though I'm not sure how much longer that will be the case.

I'd be worried more if this weren't a pattern. I'd be worried less if she had called or texted like she usually does when she's going to be late picking up John Paul.

"She's been avoiding us," Anna says. "Never a good sign."

Carla has had a series of not nice boyfriends, and her previous one was especially volatile and even violent. Each time she's in a relationship, she distances herself from us. When she first started seeing the most recent guy, she broke her pattern and not only not came around but brought him too. He seemed different and so did their relationship, but lately she had been fading away from us, which I find troubling.

"True," I say.

We pull up to the small subsidized-housing apartment complex and park in front of Minnie's unit.

Minnie and John Paul are on the front porch beneath a circle of dim illumination coming from a single porch lamp with a low-watt light bulb in it. She's in a wrinkled housecoat sitting in a white plastic chair next to a small matching table with an ashtray full of cigarette butts in it. He's playing with Sonic the Hedgehog toys on the faded-green faux turf carpet not far from her.

When John Paul sees me, he jumps up, squealing my name and running to me.

"Hey, buddy," I say. "How's it goin'?"

"Can I come to your house?"

"Sure. Let's get your toys and thank Miss Minnie."

"Do you know where my mommy is?" he asks.

"I'm gonna find her."

Anna comes up behind us.

"Anna," he squeals.

I hand him over to her, and she helps him gather his toys and loads him into his carseat in the back of the truck while I speak with Minnie.

"I'm worried, John," she says. "I am. She's never not called or texted before. Plenty of times she didn't make it back when she said she would, but she always calls or texts to let me know she'll be late."

"Any idea where she is?"

She shakes her head. "Just said she needed to do a few things, could I keep him 'til dark."

"Okay," I say. "I'll let you know when I find her. And please let me know if she contacts you."

CHAPTER
FOUR

WITH ANNA LOOKING after John Paul in the truck, I step over to Carla's unit.

Lifting the small porcelain Saint Francis statue, I thumb the dials to the correct combination, open the key safe, and remove the key.

"You didn't have to do all that," Minnie says. "There's one under the mat."

I lift the welcome mat, see the key beneath it, frown, and shake my head. When I had gotten her the Saint Francis statue key safe, I had emphasized the importance of using it exclusively, and she had promised me she would.

It's so hot my clothes are already damp with my sweat. I wipe at my forehead with my sleeve.

Unlocking and entering her apartment, I step inside and look around.

Beneath the scent of a plug-in air freshener, the small tile-floored unit has that smell most older apartments do—the lingering odors and aromas of previous tenants that never quite go away.

Carla and John Paul's home is neither clean nor neat. Toys and clothes are strewn about in the living room, bedrooms, and bathroom. Plates with food remnants are on the dining table and next to canned goods and other groceries that fill the kitchen countertops instead of the cupboard.

It's as bad as I've ever seen it, but it's still not horrible. It's far more cluttered than it is dirty, and the food left on plates appears to be recent—most likely from earlier today.

I quickly but carefully examine each room.

It's obvious this is the apartment of someone raised in poverty who had never had much or been taught to care for what she had. She has more of everything than she needs—more clothes and food and furniture and toys and even cleaning supplies that she clearly doesn't use. It's as if she fears running out so always gets extra and never says no when someone offers her anything.

It doesn't take me long to look around the tiny two-bedroom, one bathroom apartment and conclude that there's no evidence of foul play and no clues as to her whereabouts.

Before leaving, I pause and pull out my phone.

I quickly check the social media sites she uses for any info about where she might be, what she might be doing, and who she might be doing it with.

The only post she has made today is a meme of a young woman in a bathrobe being pampered at a spa with the caption "Sometimes moms need indulging too."

Going back a few days I see who she has been hanging out with and where she has been. I also see that her new relationship is now Facebook official.

Of the people showing up in her recent feed, I only have the number for one—Bailey Bozeman, a large, loud, irreverent, often obnoxious young woman with thick curly blond hair and lots and lots of it.

I search through my contacts and tap her name.

"New phone, who dis?" is how she answers.

"It's John Jordan."

"John fuckin' Jordan," she says. "Who died and am I suspect or a witness?"

"I'm lookin' for Carla," I say. "Have you seen her?"

"Haven't seen that hooker in a day or two," she says. "She's all Lady Gaga for some new dude. Ain't got any time for me."

I assume she's referring to Mason Hayes, Carla's recent and now Facebook-official relationship.

"Have any idea where she is?"

"Not the faintest."

"Would you mind tryin' to call her and asking around to see if anyone has seen her? Ask her to call me if you get her."

"Only if you deputize my ass," she says. "And put me on the pig payroll."

I wait.

She laughs. "I'm just fuckin' with you. I'll track that slut down."

"And can you send me Mason's number and those of anyone else she's been hanging out with lately?"

"I might be persuaded to do something like that . . . if . . . you give me one of those Get Out of Jail Free cards for the next time I get popped by the po-po."

CHAPTER
FIVE

"HAVE YOU HEARD FROM CARLA LATELY?" I ask.

I'm in my home office, having stepped away from game night to make a few calls out of earshot of John Paul.

"Not since this mornin'," Rudy, her dad, says. "Why?"

He's not slurring his words yet, but there is a thickness to his voice and the slow, careful over-pronunciation of someone trying not to sound impaired.

"Just tryin' to find her."

From our living room I can hear intermittent eruptions of laughter, shrieks, and squeals coming from our kids, and I'm anxious to get back in there as quickly as possible.

"She missin'?"

His words sound almost accusatory, as if it would be my fault if she were.

Rudy and I had always had a strained relationship. In addition to the guilt of his alcoholic actions and his non-actions as an absentee father, there's the perceived threat I represent as a surrogate father figure for Carla. And the strain and hostility only increased and deepened when, during Hurricane Michael, he placed John Paul and my girls in jeopardy.

"She's runnin' a little late to pick up John Paul," I say. "Just tryin' to make sure she's okay."

"Your cop brain makes you paranoid," he says. "She's probably just off havin' a good time. She deserves that occasionally, you know? Stop worryin' so much. You need me to come get my grandson?"

"No," I say. "I'll let you know when I find her."

I end the call and roll my shoulders, trying to shrug off my anger and annoyance.

I then open Bailey Bozeman's text and tap Mason Hayes's contact.

It rings several times then goes to voicemail.

Going back to her text, I look through the other contacts she sent me. Among some of the young women who had popped up in her social media feed is her ex, Easton Stevens, and I wonder why she has included him.

I then call Will Hayes, who is Mason's dad, my high school classmate, and our town's dentist.

"Hey, John," he says. "How are you?"

"I'm okay. How are you?"

"I'm great. At a dental conference at UF in Gainesville, which has been very laid back and relaxing. Just what I needed."

"I'm looking for Mason," I say. "Haven't been able to get him to answer his phone. Any idea where he is?"

"No, but I'm sure Beth does. Is something wrong?"

"I'm actually looking for Carla, and I'm hoping he knows where she is."

"Gotcha. Let me try him and Beth. I'll have Mason call you ASAP."

"Thanks."

I look back through the contacts Bailey sent me and send a few texts identifying myself and asking if any of them knows where Carla is.

I'm about to call Merrill when Will calls back.

"Hey, John. Beth said she thinks Mason is on the river and

probably doesn't have any signal. We both tried him too and couldn't get him. Carla could be with him and not have any signal either. I wish there was something I could do. I hate that I'm down here and unable to help."

"Do you know where on the river he is?"

"No, but more than likely at our little cabin. I'm sure I can get someone to go check."

Will and Beth's cabin, like most of the camps on the river, is only accessible by boat.

"That's okay," I say. "If I don't hear from her soon, I'll go check on them."

"You remember where it is?"

"On the Miccosukee, right?"

"Yeah. Let me know if I can do anything else. I can cut my trip short and come back in the morning if need be."

"Thanks, Will, but I'm sure that won't be necessary. I'll let you know."

"Please let me know what you find out," he says. "Just want to know they're safe."

"JOHN," Anna calls from the living room.

"Daddy," Taylor yells. "COME ON. IT'S YOUR TURN."

CHAPTER
SIX

AS WE'RE WRAPPING up game night, Anna leans over and says softly, "I'm sorry for how I acted earlier."

"Me too," I say.

"Thanks for making everything work. I'll take care of baths and bed. You go find Carla."

It's getting late, there's still been no word from her, and the likelihood of something being wrong is increasing with each minute that passes.

"Thank you," I say.

She turns to the kids. "Who's ready for a slumber party with John Paul?"

"I get to sleep over?" John Paul says.

"Yes, you do," Anna says. "We'll make a pallet in Taylor's room. But first . . . who wants a bedtime snack?"

"I do. I do."

I give everyone a hug, tell them I love them, then head toward my truck.

Inside my truck, I try Mason and Easton again. Still no answer.

When we end the call, I check in with Minnie and Bailey via text.

Neither of them have heard anything from Carla.

As I'm responding to them, a call comes in from a number I don't recognize.

I answer it. "John Jordan."

"Mr. Jordan, it's Cedrica Myers."

Cedrica Myers is a young African-American woman who works at city hall. I played basketball with her dad in high school.

"Hey, Cedrica. How are you?"

"I'm good, sir. How are you?"

"I'm doing okay."

"I heard you were looking for Carla Pearson," she says.

"Sure am."

"She drives that gray Camry that has her and her son's initials on the back window and the dent in the back bumper, right?"

"That's right."

"Well, I saw her car parked at the end of the road earlier this evening when we was coming off the river. Just thought I should let you know."

"Thank you," I say. "That's very helpful. I sure appreciate it. You have a good night."

"You too," she says. "And I hope you find her."

After finishing with Cedrica, I call Merrill and tell him what's going on.

"I'll grab a boat and meet you at the landing," he says.

CHAPTER
SEVEN

THE END of the road is the place where Lake Grove Road dead-ends into the Apalachicola River. There's a large asphalt parking lot, a floating dock, a boat launch, a park with picnic pavilions, and a playground.

There are only a few vehicles in the parking lot. None of them is Carla's.

While waiting for Merrill, I look around and snap some pics of the vehicles that are in the mostly empty lot, all but one of which are trucks with boat trailers hooked to them.

I wonder if Carla's car was ever really here or if Cedrica had been mistaken.

I tap Carla's number, turn my phone on speaker-phone mode, swipe away the phone screen, and search through Carla's social media accounts again.

The call eventually goes to voicemail, and there are no updates on any of the social media platforms she uses.

When Merrill arrives, I lock my truck and climb in with him.

"If she's at a camp on the Miccosukee River," he says, "doesn't make sense that her vehicle would be here."

He's right. If she went to the Hayes's cabin on the Miccosukee River with Mason, they would've launched from Tupelo Creek, which is nearly forty miles from here.

"But . . ." he adds. "Cedrica's a smart young woman. Don't really see her sayin' Carla's vehicle was there if it wasn't."

I nod. "Yeah. They could've done what we just did. Met there and left her vehicle. She climbs in with Mason, and they drive to Tupelo Creek together. But if so . . . where is her car now? If she's back and has already picked it up, why haven't we heard from her?"

"We can check her place on the way by to see if she's there."

We'll pass her apartment complex on the way to Tupelo Creek and will be able to see if her car is back without even slowing down.

If she's back, I think I would've heard from her or Minnie or one of many people who know I'm looking for her.

"How worried are you?" he asks.

"More than I was a few hours ago."

He nods but doesn't offer trite reassurances or false promises.

We ride along in silence for a while, and as we pass Carla's apartment complex he slows down a little but doesn't need to. It's obvious her vehicle isn't there and her unit is dark.

I text Anna to let her know what we're doing then try Carla's number again.

Unlike all the times before, it goes straight to voicemail.

I wait a few moments and try her again and get the same result. After a few minutes I try it again and again, getting the same result, which leads me to conclude that it wasn't that she was on another call but that her phone has died.

"Her phone's dead," I say.

He frowns and nods.

I've been trying to decide if and when to make Carla's disappearance official and report her as missing, and I believe now is the time to get our agency involved. I have three options. I can generate a case myself, I can call dispatch, or I can call the sheriff directly. Since I don't have my laptop with me and I'm not near the substation, I can't initiate the report myself. If Reggie was still sheriff, I would've already called her, but since it's Fred Miller I decide to call dispatch.

I call dispatch and let them know what's going on and how out of character this is for Carla. I request a BOLO be put out for her, the deputy in her zone to begin to search for her and conduct a canvas, and a subpoena sent to her cell phone carrier so we can ping her phone for its location. Since we believe she's on the river, I also notify FWC and Search and Rescue so we can get more boats in the water looking for her.

"It'll take a while to get to Tupelo Creek," I say. "Don't want to give my mind the opportunity to go to darker and darker places on the way there. Tell me what's goin' on with you. How's Za?"

Zaire is Merrill's wife and a doctor at Sacred Heart in Port St. Joe.

"She's good. Things leveling off some after the worst of the pandemic. Lettin' that brain of hers work on other things."

"Such as?"

"Writing a book and adopting a kid."

I smile. "So you're going to be a daddy?"

"Not gonna take in every stray like your ass does, but, yeah, I might be about to give a small child the benefit of my wisdom and experience."

"Lucky kid," I say.

"I'm actually kinda excited about this shit."

"How's work?" I ask.

Merrill is an investigator with the Potter County Sheriff's Office where my dad is sheriff. He has the same job as me just in a different county.

"What's happenin' with—"

"That's something I've been wantin' to talk to you about," he says. "You think your pops is gonna run again?"

"Not sure," I say.

Dad is one of the oldest sheriff's in the state, but he hasn't mentioned retiring.

"I've got a lot of people asking me to run," he says.

"You should," I say. "You know he'll endorse you."

"Thing is . . . they pressurin' me to run whether he retires or not. I wouldn't even consider it, but . . . they're sayin' they gonna run somebody against him and feel like they can win—because of his age and . . ."

By *they* I'm sure he means the leadership of the Democratic Party. If Dad runs again, he'll run as a Republican, so even if he has opposition in the primary, whoever runs as a Democrat will face him in the general election. And no matter who runs in either primary, I think Dad and Merrill would win and face each other in the general—and it's possible they wouldn't even have opposition in the primaries.

He says, "Say they'd rather it be someone like me than . . . someone less qualified or . . . good-looking."

I laugh.

But the laughter quickly fades as I think about the possibility of my dad and my closest friend in a political race against each other.

"I've been lookin' for a time to talk to him about it, but I wanted to mention it to you first."

"I appreciate it," I say.

"I ain't decided anything yet, but . . ."

I nod. "I wouldn't wait to talk to him. You know how small town gossip is. It'll get back to him soon—if it hasn't already. I'm happy to talk to him if you want me to."

"I'll do it," he says. "I need to. Needs to come from me. Will try tomorrow."

CHAPTER
EIGHT

WE LAUNCH at Tupelo Creek and head down the Miccosukee toward the Hayes's camp.

Tupelo Creek is a small community of mostly mobile homes and fish camps around two landings on the Miccosukee River. The upper landing, where we launch from, is paved and more commercial than the lower, which is a smaller, more secluded one at the end of the short dirt road that connects them.

Before leaving, I took pictures of the vehicles parked at the landing just like I had at Gaskin Park.

The Miccosukee River is a tributary of the Apalachicola, veering off and cutting a seven-mile channel before rejoining the Apalachicola on route to the bay.

The river looks even more mysterious in moonlight, its twist and turns far more difficult to navigate.

The nearly full moon is so bright the surface of the water is dappled with the shadows of the canopy of cypress trees leaning inward from the damp-slick banks.

The sound of frogs, gators, crickets, cicadas, and other nocturnal creatures is so loud our boat motor can't be heard above it.

Merrill sits in back, steering the outboard motor while I sit in front holding the powerful Goodsmann handheld search light. Moving slowly, we follow the circular beam of light around downed trees and other debris in the water.

I can't help but think about all the people the river has swallowed up and refused to return and how most of them were out here at night.

Eventually, the river opens up some, its widening waters filled with fewer obstacles, and we're able to move faster.

The mid-August night is so hot and humid our shirts are soaked through in spite of the breeze produced by the speeding boat.

When we reach the Hayes's cabin we find it dark and empty, no boat moored at the little wooden dock where we tie up.

It's obvious no one is here, but I want to have a look around anyway.

Before getting out of the boat, I shine the beam of the powerful spotlight on the dock and the path leading away from it up to the cabin.

There's nothing on the old, weathered wood of the dock, but in the damp clay of the bank and in the mud of the little trail connecting the dock with the cabin there are fresh footprints.

I study the prints for a few moments. There are at least two different sets and maybe more. One looks to have been made by boots, the others by sandals or flip-flops or sneakers. The boot tracks are not only bigger but deeper, as if the person who made them is heavier than the other person or people he was with.

When I climb out of the boat onto the dock, I withdraw my phone and take pictures of the tracks on the path.

Merrill says, "'Bout all that thing is good for out here."

I nod. He's talking about using my phone as a camera because there's no cell service.

"I'm gonna take a look around," I say.

"Take your time," he says. "I'll be here."

I follow the narrow path up toward the cabin, careful not to step on the footprints already there.

The path is covered with the overhanging branches of cypress and water oak trees and bordered on both sides by tall weeds, bushes, fallen limbs, and cypress knees.

Like most of the camps on the river, the cabin is small and rustic, its boards unpainted and sun-warped.

The cabin is built up several feet on stilts for when the river floods. Up five rickety wooden steps, a screened-in porch holds three mismatched rocking chairs and a whiskey barrel table with a large pair of binoculars on it.

I shine the search light around the exterior of the cabin, then go inside.

The smell of must and mildew greets me as I open the door.

Though there are lights in the cabin, they can only be powered by a generator, which most campers bring with them when they come to their camp and take with them when they leave.

The bright handheld spotlight reveals a large open room with a random assortment of mismatched furniture. Four beds—a queen, two doubles, and a twin—are scattered throughout, their cheap headboards pressed against the walls. Around them are various chairs and tables, and in the middle of the room a couch, a loveseat, two recliners, and two high-back chairs form a circle.

In the back left corner is a simple kitchen consisting of a few wooden shelves, a short counter, an old white oven, a sink, and a couple of ice chests.

Some of the camps on the river are like second homes with all the amenities and comforts you'd expect, others like this one are old, rustic hunting and fishing cabins used mostly by men who spend most of their time in their boat if they're fishing or in the swamps if they're hunting.

I step inside and look around, open the back door, and shine the light around out back.

As in the front, there is no yard, just a small clearing. A wooden outhouse is about fifteen feet away, beyond which is a dense, nearly impenetrable river swamp.

I close up the cabin and walk back down the trail to the dock.

"Anything?" Merrill asks.

"Nothing to say for sure Carla was here tonight," I say, "but someone was. Two or three someones."

"If she was here," he says, "she wouldn't've had any signal."

"True," I say, "but why haven't we heard from her since she got back?"

"Phone could be dead."

I nod. "And why hasn't Mason called me back yet? He's clearly not here, and his vehicle wasn't at the landing, so he should have service by now."

"He ain't the only one you haven't heard back from," he says. "Suspicious Easton ain't called back either."

"Still don't know why Bailey included him."

He's about to say something when we hear the approach of another boat.

We turn to look and in another few moments can see the bright searchlight mounted on a bow and the boat behind its spill.

As they slow and pull over toward us, I can see that it's Phil and Patty, a middle-aged couple who volunteers with Search and Rescue.

Patty cuts the light, and Phil cuts the engine as they drift toward us.

"Figured we'd be the first out," Phil says. "What can we do?"

"Could you patrol up and down the river for a while just to make sure they aren't broken down somewhere?"

"You got it. The others should be here soon."

Without wasting any more time, he reverses his craft, turns, then takes off farther down river.

CHAPTER
NINE

AS WE NEAR the landing and I get cell service again, my phone vibrates in my pocket.

I pull it out to see that Ellen Messer, one of our deputies, is calling.

"Hey, Ellen," I say.

"I thought you said Mason Hayes and Carla Pearson were on the river together."

She's a gruff, middle-aged white woman with a voice that sounds like she chain smokes unfiltered cigarettes and subsists on a diet of broken glass.

"We think they may have been—earlier. Don't know for sure. Why?"

"His truck and boat are parked in his driveway," she says. "But his house is dark, and I can't get him to come to the door."

"Thanks. I'm on my way. And please keep looking for Carla."

I back the trailer down into the water, Merrill drives the boat onto it, and after securing it we are racing back toward town.

Now that I have signal again, I check my missed calls, messages, and texts.

Still no word from Carla, Mason, or Easton, but there are some missed calls from numbers I don't recognize.

I call Miss Minnie again.

It takes her a while to answer, and when she does her words are slow and her voice is thick with sleep.

"Sorry to disturb you," I say, "but I was wondering if Carla had come home yet."

"Ain't heard from her."

"Would you mind looking to see if her vehicle is back or if there are any lights on in her apartment?"

"Still ain't heard nothin' from her."

"Would you mind checking?"

"Give me a minute."

It takes her more than a minute.

"Still no sign of her," she says.

"Okay. Thanks. Please call me if you hear from her."

When I end the call, Merrill says, "Maybe they were never together."

"Would explain why he's home and she's not," I say. "Why her car was at the end of the road and he was at the cabin, but . . . the footprints indicate he wasn't alone."

CHAPTER
TEN

WILL and Beth Hayes have a huge gray and white Cape Cod style home on about ten acres near a small pond just outside of town.

The single-story gray-painted wood house is framed with wide white boards and white wooden shutters. Its steeply pitched roof features a large white stone fireplace.

Mason has a much smaller version of the same house located on the front right corner of the property near the street.

Beth's signature chili-red Mini Cooper Countryman is parked in the drive in front of her home, and it appears as if every light in the house is on, while over at Mason's place it's so dark that his gray Silverado and the trailered fishing boat hooked to it can barely be seen.

When we pull up, Ellen Messer walks over to us.

She's a middle-aged white woman with short, curly gray hair and a squarish build emphasized by her uniform.

"I've banged and banged on the doors and windows," she says in her distinctive gravelly voice.

"Okay, thanks," I say. "Keep trying. We'll check with Beth. He may be there or she may know where he is."

We pull down the drive to Beth's, hop out, and knock on her door.

"Hey, John," she says. "Merrill. Is everything okay?"

She's a mid-forties woman whose money affords her the lifestyle, products, and procedures to appear a decade younger. Her shoulder-length blond hair is pulled back into a ponytail, her big blue eyes are wide and awake, and her smooth skin is unvarnished by makeup, untouched by lines and wrinkles. Her dark-gray yoga pants and light-gray fitted muscle tank show off her firm, athletic figure.

In high school Will had been awkward and overweight, and Beth had barely noticed him—and never in a good way. When Will moved back to the area, he had grown up, shed some weight, and become a successful dentist. And Beth had noticed.

After several drinks at one of our class reunions, a friend of Beth's and a classmate of ours had explained to us that there are reachers and settlers. To her way of thinking, reachers marry out of their league and settlers marry below it. Her shallow theory was based mostly on outward, physical characteristics, but it does crudely sum up how many people see Will and Beth—including, sadly, Will and Beth.

Will pampers Beth and Mason, lavishing them with an indulged lifestyle few can fathom, and in return he expects allegiance, loyalty, and for them to follow his rules.

"We're looking for Mason," I say.

"Yeah, Will called and told me you were. I saw him briefly when he came in and told him to call you. Did he not?"

"He did not," I say. "Is he at his house? We can't get him to come to the door."

"Yeah. Let me call him. I can't believe he didn't call you."

She turns and disappears down the hallway. When she returns, she's on her phone.

"Honey, the police are here. I thought you were going to call them."

She waits.

"Oh," she says. "Well . . . Okay. But . . . Your father told you to call John. Well, but . . . you can talk to them now."

She lifts the phone from her mouth, looks at us, and says, "He fell asleep."

When she moves the phone back to her mouth, she says, "Meet them at your door. I'm sending them down there now. Don't fall back asleep. Get up now, okay? Okay."

CHAPTER
ELEVEN

"SORRY," Mason is saying. "I fell asleep."

He rubs his eyes and yawns in what seems like attempts to bolster his assertion that he has been asleep.

He's leaning in his doorway, his head down, not making eye contact with us.

He's wearing a pair of blue jeans with no shirt, his pale, thin upper body on display. There's a little definition as if he spends some time working out, but he's so skinny it barely registers.

"Where have you been tonight?" I ask.

"Huh? Why?"

His hair is longish and unkempt and obscures much of his downturned face.

"Why what?" I ask. "Are you unwilling to answer my questions? Is there some reason you don't want to tell me where you've been?"

"No, but . . . I know my rights. I haven't done anything wrong. I'm not gonna be harassed. I just asked why you wanted to know where I've been. If I ask you where you've been, wouldn't you want to know why?"

Though his attitude is defiant, his voice remains calm and pleasant in a good ol' boy kind of way.

"Maybe we should finish this conversation at the sheriff's office," I say.

"Not unless you're arresting me."

The low rumbling of thunder rolls in the distance, early warnings of an approaching storm.

"So you're refusing to answer our questions and refusing to come to the station?"

"Look, all I've done is ask why you're interrogating me. I have a right to know."

Merrill says, "This is nothing like an interrogation. Promise you that."

I say, "I'm asking because I'm looking for Carla. She's missing."

"*Missing*?"

"Yeah."

"She's ain't missin'. She's late as usual or laid up drunk somewhere, but she ain't *missin'*."

"Carla doesn't drink," I say. "You know that. Do you know where she is?"

He shakes his head. "I do not."

"Any ideas where she might be?"

He shakes his head and shrugs.

The distant thunder rolls again, this time followed by the flickering of lightning on the horizon.

"Have you seen her?"

"'Course I've seen her in the past, but you're lookin' for her now, and I don't know where she is now."

The longer we speak, the more drawl he adds to his southern accent. He uses it as camouflage to hide his intelligence and to sound affable and folksy.

"When was the last time you saw her?" I ask.

He shrugs. "I'll have to think about it."

"Was it today?"

He nods slowly. "Yeah, guess I saw her today."

"When? Where? Where was the last time and place you saw

her?"

He shrugs.

"Is there a reason you're being so vague and uncooperative?" I ask.

"I'm not," he says. "I'm just not gonna be pushed around 'cause you got a gun and a badge and a . . ." He looks at Merrill.

"Did you hurt her?" Merrill asks.

"*What*? No."

"Where is she?" Merrill says.

"I told you that I don't know."

"Where was she the last time you saw her?" he asks.

My phone vibrates, and I pull it out and glance at it. It's Mason's dad, Will. I answer it.

"Beth said Mason never called you," he says. "I'm so sorry. I . . . Sometimes that boy . . . We were too easy on him growing up. Have you spoken to him yet?"

"Trying to now—"

"Sorry, didn't mean to interrupt."

"No, it's not that. He's refusing to cooperate."

Will lets out a frustrated and disgusted sigh. "Would you mind putting me on speaker phone?"

I do.

"Mason," Will says. "I'm gonna listen in while you answer John's questions. We need to do everything we can to help him find Carla. I hope you're doing that—everything you can, I mean. If I feel like you're not . . . I can tell you that your lifestyle is about to change very drastically. Understand?"

Mason stands up straighter and says, "Yes, sir."

The approaching storm is closer, the thunder growing louder and more ominous, the lightning making electrical etchings in the night sky.

"Did you see Carla today?" I ask.

"Yes, sir," he says, making eye contact for the first time.

"Where?"

"End of the road."

"When was this?" I ask.

"Not sure exactly. Late afternoon, I guess."

"Was she with anyone?"

"No, sir."

"What did y'all do?" I ask.

"Talked for a little while. Just kinda . . . feelin' things out. We've been . . . We haven't been gettin' along, so . . . Wasn't sure if we were . . ."

"Then what?"

"We sorta patched things up."

"Then?"

"She got in the truck with me, and we went for a ride."

The storm is still in the distance, but its effect on the atmosphere are palpable. It feels like the bottom has fallen out of the barometric pressure.

"Where'd you go?" I ask.

"Nowhere."

Will clears his throat on the phone.

Mason glances at the phone and leans in toward it a little. "I mean nowhere in particular," Mason says toward the phone, "just rode around a little."

"Then?"

"Then I took her back to her car."

"Then?" I ask.

Will says, "Son, quit making him ask you what happened next over and over. Just tell him everything."

"Yes, sir. I . . . She . . . We decided to go on the river. She followed me in her car, 'cause I was planning on stayin' longer than her. She had to pick up her kid. I launched the boat at Tupelo Creek. She left her car there. We rode down the river, eventually went to our cabin. We were just gonna fool around and chill. Nothin' big. But we started fighting—well, I mean fussing. Nothing physical. Just words—arguing and whatnot. Told her I had enough and was leaving. She went crazy. I mean really nuts. Yelling and screaming and crying and acting all psycho. Told her I wasn't puttin' up with that shit anymore. Said I was leaving. Told her I'd take her back to her car. But she wasn't havin' any of it. I said 'get your crazy ass in the boat or you're gettin' left.' She refused, so I left."

"Without her?" I ask.

"Yeah."

Will says, "You left Carla out there all alone?"

"I told her I'd take her to her car," he says. "I . . . She's the one who wouldn't get in the boat."

"You marooned her out there with no way to get back in," Will says.

"I told her to get in the boat. She wouldn't. Figured she'd flag down a passing boat and get a ride in. She just didn't want to ride with me."

"We were just at the cabin," I say. "She wasn't there."

"Well . . . She musta gotten a ride. Like I said. Was her car at the landing?"

I shake my head.

"See? She got a ride in with someone else."

"Then where is she?" I ask. "Why can't anyone find her? Why hasn't she picked up her son? She never leaves him this long—not without letting the babysitter know she'll—"

"She knows you'll always get him," he says.

"Mason," Will says, "I can't believe you left her out there."

"What was I supposed to do?"

"Almost anything else. Smooth things over so she would ride with you. Wait with her until someone came by she could ride with and follow them in to make sure she was safe. Take care of her—even if you were arguing, even if it was the last thing you'd ever do for her."

"You really don't know where she is now?" I ask.

"No, sir, I don't."

"We're gonna need you to come in and give us a formal statement," I say.

Will says, "If I find out you left anything out or did anything else you're not tellin' us, I'll do far worse to you than the law will. Do you understand me? I didn't raise you to be like this."

But, of course, we all know that this is exactly what Will and Beth had raised him to be like—spoiled, self-centered, narcissistic, sexist, and maybe even a little sociopathic.

CHAPTER
TWELVE

"YOU BELIEVE HIM?" Merrill asks.

I shrug. "Not inclined to."

While Ellen Messer takes Mason in, we are racing back toward Tupelo Creek, trying to beat the storm. When we get there, we will launch the boat as quickly as possible and look for Carla at the Hayes's cabin.

"Be good to get him on record," I say, "and see what a VSA says about what he's saying."

A VSA or voice stress analyzer is software that detects deception in the human voice by measuring vocal micro tremors and other psychological signs—both verbal and nonverbal—that indicate falsity. It's just one of many tools we use to try to get to the truth when investigating a case.

Though we're in Merrill's personal truck, it is equipped with an emergency light bar, which he has on. He's driving about as fast as the truck pulling the boat can handle. Fortunately, there's very little traffic on the pine-tree-lined rural highway.

Merrill says, "Wonder how much he left out and how much is out and out lies?"

"Leaving her stranded on the river is such an awful admission," I say. "Either it's the truth or he did something far worse."

Merrill nods. "It being the truth is best case."

Merrill used to shift between standard American English formal register and a kind of ebonics-laced street language with greater frequency than he does now, and I realize how much I miss it. He's still fully capable of it, just utilizes it far more judiciously these says. It's probably partly related to growing up and to his professional position with the Potter County Sheriff's Office, but it's probably mostly because of his marriage to Za. Of course, tonight he's less playful in general—both out of concern for Carla and care for me.

I think about the fact that Carla's car wasn't at the landing and what it might mean. It could support Mason's statement. Maybe Carla was able to flag down a passing boat and get a ride back in. It's unlikely. There's not a lot of traffic on this river at any particular time and almost none at all on a Sunday night. And if she was able to get back to her vehicle, where is she and why hasn't she returned any of our calls? But if Mason took it somewhere to cover up something he had done, who helped him? How'd he get back to his vehicle, and where did he hide it?

The storm is behind us, stalking us like a predator who knows its prey can't get away, moving slowly but relentlessly and with a sense of inevitability.

I look at my phone and wonder again why I haven't heard back from any of the contacts Bailey had given me. I also wonder again why she included Easton.

I call dispatch to see if anything has turned up on her vehicle or the BOLO, but nothing has.

I then do the same with the deputies, investigators, and Search and Rescue. So far no one has turned up anything.

I tell everyone what Mason said happened and about Carla's car being missing from the landing.

We only have Mason's word that Carla's car was ever at the landing, but the fact that Cedrica saw it at the end of the road and it not being there when we were there could support his story. The fact that it's no longer at Tupelo Creek means that she's most likely not still on the river, at the cabin, or in the swamp. Our time might be better spent searching somewhere else, but I have to go back out there in case she's still there. I have to try to find her, and I don't know what else to do or where else to look.

I then request an additional deputy to canvas the landing and the area around it to see if anyone actually saw Carla or her vehicle.

Next I call Michelle Quinn, our crime scene investigator, to see if she can go with us to the Hayes's cabin.

My phone vibrates, and I glance at it. Will Hayes is calling.

"Hey, John," he says. "I wanted to apologize to you again for how Mason was acting earlier. Please let me know if he gives you any more attitude, and I'll get involved again. I didn't raise him to be like that, to do any of this."

"Thanks. I will."

"Also wanted you to know I'm headed back tonight, and I want to help in any way I can. Just let me know what I can do. Hopefully you'll have found her by the time I get back, but if not I can help search. Mason can too in his boat. That's give us—"

"We've impounded his truck and boat," I say.

"Really? Why?"

"To search and process it," I say.

"Oh my God. You don't think . . . He couldn't have . . . Mason's spoiled, but he's no . . . He wouldn't have . . . hurt her."

"I hope you're right," I say. "We'll know soon enough."

"I truly believe he's incapable of anything violent," he says. "I really and sincerely do, but if he did anything—*anything* at all —he will accept the consequences of his actions. I'll see to that. I just can't believe it will come to that. It can't."

CHAPTER
THIRTEEN

THIS TIME when we head down the Miccosukee River, crime scene investigator Michelle Quinn is in the boat with us.

She's a thin, mid to late twenties African-American woman with a short afro and striking, enormous eyes so black as to seem pupilless. She's dressed in a raincoat, khakis, and Gore-Tex waterproof hiking boots.

This trip down the river is far more treacherous than the previous one, and as lightning strikes backlight the cypress, red maple, river birch, and tupelo trees lining the dark, giant serpent snaking toward the bay, I wonder if I was wrong to bring her.

I had asked her to join us primarily to help with the footprints.

Technically, the cabin isn't a crime scene yet, and my hope is that it doesn't become one. If it does, FDLE will be called in, and its crime scene unit will process it. But between now and then I don't want us to miss anything or destroy any potential evidence, and I'd like to know what the footprints can tell us.

To my eyes there were possibly three sets of footprints, but I want to know what Michelle thinks and see if she can help interpret and preserve them.

It rained earlier and damaged or destroyed many of the

prints, but I'm hoping enough of them remain to assist us in locating Carla—and Michelle gives us our best chance at that.

As evidence, footprints can establish a link between victim, suspect, and crime scene, show how many people were present at the scene at the time of occurence, approximate the stature, gait pattern, and movement of potential suspects and victims, and reveal the material, model, and size of the footwear, but all I want them to do is help us find Carla.

The wind that has arrived just before the storm has the trees and bushes on the banks whipping around and waving, putting a frenetic chop on the surface of the water that causes the river to look like the bay.

When we reach the cabin, Michelle quickly creates and flags a path for us to use based on the one I had used before.

She then begins to photograph the prints using a Canon camera on a tripod.

"Not sure how much I can do before the storm gets here," she yells over the wind, "but I'll get as much as I can of what I think could be the most useful."

As the storm gets closer, the elongated, explosive expansions of the thunder that sound like an echoing electrical growl change into shorter, more staccato bursts of snaps, bangs, and cracks.

In general, there are three types of footprints—visible, latent, and plastic.

Visible prints are imprints produced by dust, particles, or stains stuck on the sole of feet or footwear. Latent prints are invisible to the naked eye and are typically the most abundant but also the most vulnerable. Plastic prints are three dimensional prints usually found on a pliable surface such as mud or snow.

The flash from Michelle's camera mimics the lightning strikes behind us.

In addition to photography, Michelle will likely use some of the other methods of collecting and preserving prints—lifting, gelatin filters, Electrostatic Dust, and casting.

Photography is the most commonly used method. Adhesive

lifters, which are used on smooth surfaces like tiles, metal counters, hardwood surfaces, will probably only be used on the dock and in the cabin. Gelatin filters will be used if any impressions are found on porous surface or irregular surfaces, and they consist of a rubber sheet with a layer of adhesive gelatin on one side. They are more flexible than adhesive lifters.

Electrostatic dust is a tool that electrostatically charges the particles present in the dust or soil, which get attracted and then collected on the lifting film, but this is primarily used for dry impressions, which we probably won't have here. Finally, casting uses plaster of paris, paraffin wax, or sulfur to collect three dimensional footprints, which because of the muddy ground we should have plenty of here.

We help Michelle get started, assisting her by holding lights, assembling casting frames, and mixing up the casting material.

The fences or casting frames are small, lightweight, adjustable frames made of aluminum that serve as a form to hold the casting material in place. The casting material she uses is Crime-Cast, a complete plaster casting mixture in a single bag, which includes water.

Once we've helped her all we can, we look around the cabin again while she casts some of the prints.

In addition to looking at everything even more closely than before, I intermittently call out for Carla, letting her know I'm here and it's safe to come out.

Eventually, Michelle shouts to us, and we go back out front.

"I'm ready to look around with you," she yells over the wind. "I just wanted to preserve what I could in case it rains again."

"Thanks."

"Hopefully we won't need them, but we'll have them if we do. It's a real mess. The path is so narrow mostly the footprints are on top of each other—and the rain did a fair bit of damage, but . . . I was able to get photos of everything and a few casts."

I nod. "Good. Thank you."

"I'd need to spend more time with it—and do it during

daylight—to be sure about everything, but we just don't have it, and I feel like finding her is the priority now. Best I can tell there are three to five different prints. If I had to guess I'd say maybe three male and two female, but that's just a guess. Like I say, there may only be three total. If that's the case, then I'd say two male and one female. I can't be sure, but again a quick guess is the path shows the males entering and returning but the female only entering. Or if there are two females then one entering and returning and one only entering. That's why I'd like to follow these on up to the cabin and beyond if they go anywhere else."

"We'll follow you," I say.

She carries her camera and flashlight and leads the way. Merrill and I follow carrying the rest of her equipment.

The trail we're traversing goes from dark with only small circles of flashlight beams on it to brilliantly overexposed when the lighting flashes, and my dilating pupils can't keep up.

She walks on the flagged path beside the trail, stepping on my footprints from earlier tonight and mine and Merrill's from a short while before.

As she moves, she examines the trail with her flashlight, pausing occasionally to take pictures.

"All the prints lead to the cabin," she yells. "The path widens some here as it reaches the cabin. I can probably get some better images and casts here. Okay for us to stop for a few minutes for me to see what I can get? I'll be quick."

"Sure."

We wait and assist her while she works.

I'm anxious to continue, but I know what she gathers now could become very useful later. I just hope we won't need it, that we'll locate Carla safe and unharmed and that will be the end of this.

I'm trying not to think about it, but every moment that passes makes it that much more likely that Carla is not okay.

When Michelle finishes, we continue.

"So they all lead to the cabin," she yells. "And some lead

back down the path to the dock. Is someone or a couple of some-ones still here or were their footprints trampled by the others and removed by the rain?"

"No one is in the cabin," I say, "but there are footprints out back."

"Let's take a look at them while we still can. I can process the cabin while it's stormin'."

Instead of walking through the cabin and out the back door, we walk around the side, examining the ground as we do.

"So anyone who had to use the bathroom had to come out here," Michelle yells, shining her light on the ground between the cabin and the outhouse. "And it looks like they all did."

She moves along the short, narrow trail between the cabin and outhouse and we follow. "Look at that," she shouts. "The same prints that don't seem to return to the dock out front seem to veer off this little trail to the outhouse. See?" She trains the beam of her flashlight onto the set of prints that walk around to the side of the outhouse and then into the swamp. "Can't be sure that's Carla, but I'd bet my house that it's a girl in flip-flops or sandals."

"That's what she normally wears," I yell.

The wind picks up even more, and the first raindrops begin to pelt us—large, driving drops that sting the skin like a slap and leave a prominent wet spot.

"Can't imagine she went very far into the swamp—and if she did, there won't be prints for very long—the ground's too wet—but we can follow the prints if you want to."

"I want to," I yell. "Let's see what we can find before the storm washes it all away."

"We need to get the dogs out here," Merrill yells.

I nod.

"Follow me," Michelle yells. "Stay close. And try not to get struck by lightning."

CHAPTER
FOURTEEN

"THAT'S IT," Michelle yells.

She's pointing to the final footprint, a partial, the back part of which is in damp sand, the front part of which disappears into the standing water of what looks to be a seepage wetland—a part of the swamp where water oozes onto the surface from the ground water aquifer.

"I can't say she didn't go farther in, and I can't say she didn't come out," she says. "There's just nothing else to go on. The terrain is too . . . wet."

"And about to get wetter," Merrill says. "We've got to get back to the cabin."

The rain is falling steadily now and becoming harder by the moment.

"Y'all head back to the cabin," I say. "I'm gonna look a little longer then meet you there."

"Come back with us," Merrill says. "I'll come back out with you as soon as the storm passes."

"It's not gonna pass anytime soon," I say. "I won't be long. Get her back to the cabin safely, and I'll be right behind you."

"It's too easy to get lost in the swamp when it's not storming," he says. "In this . . . you'll get lost in no time and . . . you won't be able to see or hear anything anyway."

"I can't stop looking for her," I say. "Not yet."

He nods. "Okay."

"I'll see y'all back there in a little while."

He grabs Michelle's equipment and ushers her back the way we came.

"Be careful," she yells over her shoulder. "Come back soon. We'll help you search after the storm."

I glance at the disappearing footprint again and try to determine the direction she was headed.

This part of the river swamp is dense, thick understory growth beneath ancient oak trees.

I press through the bushes, my boots getting sucked down into the mud with every step.

Within seconds of the rain arriving in earnest, I'm drenched, my clothes soaked through the same as if I had fallen in the river.

I squint against the rain running into my eyes.

The wind is shaking the trees so violently that there seems to be as many leaves as raindrops falling from the sky above.

Lightning is popping all around me, the thunder clap that follows it so close as to seem simultaneous.

With one hand I attempt to shield my face from the rain and the sand and twigs and bits of bark and debris the wind is hurling about, while with the other I attempt to push back the bushes and other obstacles in my way.

I pause occasionally to shine the flashlight in front of me, but it's so dark and the rain is so heavy that I'm mostly having to feel my way around. I'd use the lightning strikes to see, but they're so quick and brilliant that they cause momentary blindness.

As I move about I call out to Carla and attempt to listen for a reply, but my voice is immediately lost in the whirlwind of the storm. There's no way she could hear me over the wind and rain and thunder, and there's no way I could hear her reply.

Merrill's right. It's absolutely absurd to be out here in this—the futility only matched by the danger, but I can't stop searching for her. I can't be safe and dry in the cabin knowing she could be out here.

I not only feel responsible for Carla and feel like I let her down when I moved and didn't reach out to her as much as I should have, but I still feel guilty about something I did following Hurricane Michael.

Carla had been babysitting Johanna and Taylor along with John Paul at her place the morning of the day that changed everything—the day Michael made landfall. Rudy, her father, had stopped by, and when she feel asleep he loaded all three kids into his car and headed to Mexico Beach to evacuate his brother before the storm arrived. He took our children and drove them directly into the path of the storm. They were all there at ground zero when the super storm hit. Rudy's brother had been killed, and Rudy left our daughters alone in peril while fleeing with John Paul. I had found Johanna and Taylor moments before they would've died. We barely survived. When night fell, I had momentarily chosen to take Johanna and Taylor home instead of staying and continuing to search for Rudy and John Paul. I had changed my mind and gone back and eventually found him, but I had never forgiven myself for those few minutes of leaving him —and neither had Carla.

As I feel my way through the storm-seized swamp, I recall Carla's words to me.

"Would you leave if they were missing?" Carla had asked me, nodding toward the girls. "Think about what you just did to find them."

"I did that for John Paul too," I say.

"But you haven't found him yet. Why are you quitting?"

"I'm not," I say. "I'll be back in the morning with more help. But

there's nothing else we can do tonight. There's no electricity. It's dark and dangerous—"

"You wouldn't let danger stop you lookin' for them."

"I don't mean dangerous for me," I say. *"I mean for John Paul or others out there. Do you realize how easy it would be to run over someone or bump into a pile of debris and crush someone under or near it? Search and rescue operations will start tomorrow. Professionals who know what they're doing will be looking for him."*

"Well, I can't leave," she had said, *"and you shouldn't be able to either."*

But I had been able to—for a few minutes. I had gotten into a truck with Merrill and Anna and our girls, and I had started for home before turning back around and going back to be with Carla and help her find her son.

I never should have temporarily stopped searching for John Paul. I can never stop searching for Carla. No matter what. No matter how dangerous. No matter how futile. No matter how long it takes.

CHAPTER
FIFTEEN

"CARLA," I yell.

I'm stumbling around the swamp, soaking wet, exhausted, disoriented, lost.

I have no idea where I am.

My throat is weak and hoarse from yelling. My eyes are irritated and scratchy and, ironically, dry—the only dry thing about me besides my mouth. My head is throbbing, and the dread I feel has made its way down into my body.

The last of the storm is fading, only scattered raindrops and random gusts of wind remaining.

The night is darker now, the moon obscured by a black blanket of thick clouds.

"CARLA."

I think about Reggie and what I wish I could've done for her. I'm still grieving for her, the wounds her leaving left still open and raw. I can't lose Carla too. I just can't.

I crest a slight incline and find myself looking down at a narrow, dry slough bed. The small tributary which is full of water when the river floods is now just a muddy mess.

I know I can follow it back to the river, and I will, eventually, but I want to look around some more first.

I walk away from the slough, slowly feeling my way through the dark, wet jungle-like world—of which I seem the sole inhabitant.

My phone battery has only seventeen-percent charge remaining, and I'm trying to use it sparingly.

I haven't gotten very far back down the ridge when I trip over a cypress knee and land on the wet ground next to a crayfish chimney, the aboveground borough looking like a large stack of melted marshmallows glowing ghostly in the low light.

When I stand, I walk another fifty feet or so, stop and shine my light around in every direction.

To my left is a stand of thin cypress trees, their narrow trunks above their bulging bases resembling arthritic fingers reaching up to the rust-colored leaves above, their knees mostly hidden in the green and brown sagebrush-looking vegetation below.

To my right is a short, winding slough, either end of which is cutoff from a water supply. The standing black water is lined with exposed and tangled root systems of cypress, tupelo, and pond pine trees reaching toward the water.

All around and in between the wet ground like a kind of algal muck filled with the detritus of dead and shed plant and animal matter—one area of which serves as a bed for zigzag bladderwort plants.

As I move the beam about, the beauty of the swamp is revealed in small, subtle ways, dim, oddly exposed snapshots of broadleaf cattails, Virginia irises, white water lilies, black willows, spider lilies, swamp roses, lizard tails, upland chorus frogs, squirrel tree frogs, salamanders, a huge dragonfly sitting on a stalk of eastern pond hawk.

Eventually, I continue on, calling out for Carla as I do.

I also continue to stumble, trip, and fall—the worst of which is when I trip over the exposed roots of a tupelo tree and fall into the small body of standing water next to it, both my phone and my flashlight getting submerged in the dark water. Jumping up,

I dry them off as best I can on my wet shirt, and for the moment they seem to still be working.

As I futilely search the swamp for Carla, I think back to the time when I discovered she was keeping her newborn at Rudy's Diner while she worked the night shift, mother and child sleeping at the counter between waiting on customers.

I look down at the good-natured little baby boy with the enormous brown eyes who just a few short months ago was going to be my son, and feel, as I always do, a complex mix of sadness and joy, regret, longing, and love.

Sliding my hands behind him and easing him out of his car seat, I say, "Let's let your mama sleep a little more. Whatta you say?"

I lift him to me, kissing his forehead and gently placing his head on my shoulder, rocking him in my arms and patting his back.

I couldn't love him any more if he were my own son.

"You're so good with him," Carla says. "I feel so guilty for not . . . for keeping him."

I look away so she can't see me, pretending to be adjusting John Paul in my arms, and blink my stinging eyes.

"There's no world," I say when I can, "in which you should feel guilty for keeping your own child. Please let that go. You have absolutely nothing to feel guilty about. You did nothing wrong. You did everything right."

I mean what I'm saying. She did nothing wrong. And of course she should keep her baby. But that doesn't change the fact that the entire experience has been complicated and painful for me and for Anna. For months before he was born, we thought he was going to be ours. We rushed Carla to the hospital, worried the baby was coming too early, concerned for his and her safety and believing he was ours. We stayed with him in the hospital for weeks, taking care of him in his vulnerable, premature condition and helping his mom physically and emotionally, believing he was ours.

For months we believed we had another child. It didn't matter to us whether he was a boy or a girl; we were just happy to welcome another child into our home. It didn't matter that he was a boy, but it was significant. Years and years ago I had a dream of being at the beach with my little boy. A dream I truly believed had finally come true.

Anna and I had something we were no longer able to have on our own—a baby—a child together. And then Carla changed her mind. It would have been difficult under any circumstances, but for us to have him, care for him, receive him into our family only to have him snatched away, taken from us, had been only slightly less emotionally devastating than if he had been kidnapped or succumbed to SIDS.

"I'm sorry for getting your hopes up and . . ."

"You didn't," I lie. "You didn't do anything wrong. Our family is complete. It's not like Anna or I feel like we have to have a son or that we're incomplete without a boy somehow. It's not the case. Not at all. We love our girls, and they are more than enough. We feel like the luckiest parents in the world. We were going to take him because you asked us to, because you needed us to, and we would have loved him like our own—we still do—but we weren't actively looking for another child. You didn't do anything wrong."

She gives me a sleepy smile. "You're almost convincing."

"Even if you thought you got our hopes up and that we were disappointed when we didn't get him, you have nothing to feel guilty for. He's your baby. You made the right decision."

"I feel guilty . . . I feel guilty because y'all could give him a better life than I can," she says.

I shake my head. "Absolutely not. No one can give him a better life than you can. And we're going to help you—as much as you'll let us—give him the best life you possibly can."

So far she has been unwilling to let us do much of anything for him or for her, and I think I know why.

"You really think he's better off with me?"

"His own mother?" I say. "Of course. Absolutely."

"And you're not mad at me?"

"Of course not," I say. "We love you. We want you in our lives. Want you to let us do more for you and your baby."

She nods and gives me something between a smile and a frown.

"Are you not letting us help because of the guilt you mentioned?" I ask. "Or because you think we might try to take him from you?"

Tears appear in her eyes. "I'd never think you guys would try to take my baby from me," she says, "but . . . y'all are so good with him, with your girls, and I fuckin' suck as a mother, and . . . it just points out how good y'all are and how bad I am and how selfish I'm being not to let y'all raise him."

"Oh, Carla," I say. "You're a great mother and you're not being selfish. He's your child. You can't be selfish with your child. Something would be wrong if you didn't want him."

"I knew you wouldn't try to take him, but I did think that others would see how much better y'all are than me and report it to Children and Family Services and they'd take him away from me and give him to you."

"Would never happen," I say. "Not in a million years. You have nothing to worry about. And nobody thinks you're a bad mom or that we would be better. No one. And there wouldn't be anything to compare. It wouldn't be like we'd have him and then you'd have him and someone could compare the two. We're just wanting to help you with him. We'd be doing it together."

She starts crying. "I . . . that sounds so good. I . . . could really use some help. I feel like I'm going crazy. I'm so tired all the time, and I'm having some crazy ass thoughts."

"Like DCF taking your baby and giving him to us?" I say.

She laughs. "Yeah, like that."

"Come home with me tonight," I say. "Stay with us until we can get you your own place. Let us help you get some sleep, some rest. Let us help you with your baby. You're his parent. And I promise you Anna and I will never try to be. But you could let us be your parents and his grandparents. How about that? That could work, couldn't it?"

She and John Paul had moved in with us that night.

We had helped her get her own place and been a real part of their lives until the string of bad boyfriends had begun. Since then our involvement with them, especially her, had been far more intermittent.

"CARLA."

She's probably not even out here. I'm probably wasting my time. I could probably be helping her more by searching somewhere else, but at least for now I can't stop stumbling through the dark calling her name.

CHAPTER
SIXTEEN

EVENTUALLY, I make my way back to the slough and follow it to the river.

I emerge from the swamp about a mile up river from the Hayes's camp and walk along the slippery bank down toward it.

When I'm a little less than half way to it, I hear a boat coming down the river behind me and stop and use my flashlight to flag it down.

It's Merrill.

He pulls near a large cypress tree that has fallen in the water, and I use it as a kind of dock to climb out and into the boat.

"Took Michelle back to the landing," he says. "Called in the K-9 unit from Gulf CI. They'll be here at first light. Checked with dispatch and Search and Rescue. Nothin's turned up so far—not on Carla or her vehicle."

He tosses me a duffel bag. "Some dry clothes in there."

I unzip it and begin to change.

"There's a brick in there to charge your phone if you need it," he says.

"I need it," I say. "Thanks."

"Pretty much everybody but Phil and Patty have packed it in

for the night. Say they'll be back out first thing in the morning if she doesn't turn up before then."

"Thanks," I say.

"Michelle processed the cabin," he says. "Said she'll have some results for us tomorrow, but at least one of the prints from outside never went into the cabin—the one that we saw when we went around it."

I nod and think about what that could mean.

"Search and Rescue says they've searched several miles up and down the river," he says, "and there's no broken down or abandoned boats and nothing suspicious."

I finish dressing, plug my phone in to charge, and thank him for the info.

"What you want us to do next?" he asks.

Before I can respond, his radio blares. It's Phil.

"We've got a fire down here," he says. "At the old McDaniel cabin. Come quick."

CHAPTER
SEVENTEEN

THE MCDANIEL PLACE IS AN OLD, rustic fish camp that has been in the McDaniel family for several decades. During Hurricane Michael, the cat 5 superstorm that ripped through the region, an enormous oak tree had fallen onto it, caving in nearly half the roof and most of one wall. Because the structure was so old and weak to begin with and because the storm dumped several months worth of rainfall into it, the camp had been condemned and is waiting to be torn down and rebuilt—neither of which has happened yet.

When we pull up to the camp, we find Phil and Patty sitting in their boat out in front of it.

"Seemed suspicious to have a fire in it on a wet night like tonight," Phil says.

I look up the incline of the bank to the cabin.

It's an old tin roof fish camp built out of mismatched lumber over a long period of time. Its unpainted boards are warped and weathered and wet. Though raised up on stilts, it's neither high enough or far enough from the river and has been flooded several times over its many years of existence. The lot it sits on is thick and overgrown and looks like what it is—abandoned.

The building itself isn't on fire, but through the cave-in

opening a fire can be seen burning in what looks like a closet in the back right corner.

The fire is small enough and back far enough that it's difficult to see from here, and I wonder how Phil and Patty saw it as they sped by.

"Yes, it does," I say. "Thanks for letting us know."

"Guess it coulda been started by a lightning strike," Phil adds, "but . . ."

"You were right to call us," I say. "We'll check it out."

I shine the spotlight around the bank and the path leading up to the camp.

A boat has been moored here recently and there are footprints leading up to the cabin.

Patty says, "We're gonna call it a night, get some sleep so we can be back out here in the morning to start searching again."

"Thank you," I say. "I really appreciate all y'all have done."

"See y'all tomorrow," Phil says.

He cranks his motor, reverses away from the bank, and then heads back up the river.

Merrill and I tie up the boat and make our way up the path, careful not to disturb the other prints in the ground.

The cloud coverage has cleared somewhat, and the huge, bright moon is visible again, making everything else more visible as well.

"Need to get Michelle back out here," Merrill says.

I nod.

The wet ground is a muddy mess, and our boots alternate between slipping and being sucked into the muck.

We have to climb over downed trees and walk around upturned root systems. If someone came to the cabin earlier and set the fire, they had to really want to do so. It's not easy to access.

When we reach the collapsed structure, Merrill hands me a pair of latex gloves, and we both glove up before entering.

Opening the crooked front door, we enter and immediately have to walk around the top of the fallen oak resting there.

The cabin is as wet as the swamp itself, every surface slick and dripping with rainwater.

The furniture in the open room is rotting and mildewed after being exposed to the elements in the years since the storm.

The fire is in a closet in the back right corner of the room on top of part of a collapsed wooden dining table. An old padded wooden glider rocker stands a few feet away from the closet, its green padding burned and charred. The closet and the chair are the only two areas to have been burned. The closet, which is empty apart from a few random hangers on the bar extended across it, is about the driest spot in the entire cabin, and is an obvious place to set a fire. But the chair is curious. Did the fire in the closet jump to the chair? It seems too far away, and if it is, why start a separate fire on it?

It's hard to tell what is burning but it looks to be trash and debris and clothes.

We look around for something to put the fire out.

Finding a couple of wet sheets and blankets, we attempt to extinguish the fire while disturbing it as little as possible.

It takes us a few minutes because of the approach we're taking, but eventually we are able to stamp out the fire.

I study the remnants of the fire.

When I confirm there's no body beneath the debris, I exhale a sigh of relief and realize I hadn't breathed deeply since we got the call that there was a fire here.

Most of whatever was in the fire is blackened and charred beyond recognition, but materials being consumed appear to be branches, leaves, some random broken wooden furniture parts and pieces, a blanket, and some clothes.

I can't tell for sure, but from the small section of clothes that are the least burned, they don't appear to be old.

I can't help but wonder if they are Carla's or Mason's or whoever did her harm—if someone did her harm.

"This wasn't from a lightning strike," Merrill says.

I nod. "Sure doesn't look like it. Definitely suspicious. And as wet as everything is a lot of accelerant would have had to be used."

"Could've been somebody sheltering during the storm," he says.

"But why not put out the fire before they left? Why have a fire at all?"

He nods.

"As much as I don't want to think it," I say. "It could be an attempt at burning evidence."

"We'll get an arson investigator and the crime scene techs out here in the morning." Merrill says. "Hopefully they'll tell us we're being paranoid and overreacting."

CHAPTER
EIGHTEEN

"JOHN, I swear to you I don't know where she is," Mason is saying.

It's a little after four in the morning. I woke him up at the jail and brought him to the interview room at the sheriff's office so I can record the interview and run what he says through the voice stress analyzer.

I have yet to sleep, and I came here straight from searching the river, but he seems more tired and sleepy than I am.

To establish a baseline of true statements for the VSA, I ask him a series of innocuous questions.

"Is your name Mason Darius Hayes?"

"Yes."

"Do you live at 747 Canning Street?"

"Yes."

"What do you do for work?"

"I'm a . . . I'm in between jobs right now."

"Is your dad the dentist in town?"

"Yes. Well, he's *a* dentist in town. I think the medical center has one too."

"Who all was out at your cabin tonight?"

"Just me and her."

"Who is her?"

"Carla. Just me and Carla."

"Footprints say different."

"Maybe somebody was out there before us or someone came by after I left," he says. "I don't know. When I was out there it was just me and her."

"I want you to really think about your answers," I say. "Be as honest and truthful as you possibly can. These are your official statements. We'll know if you're lying, and it will look very incriminating if you change or amend your statements later."

"I'm telling the truth," he says, the tone of his voice tightening and rising some. "I swear it."

"Did you hurt Carla?"

He hesitates for the briefest of moments but he definitely hesitates.

"No," he says.

"Are you sure?"

"I'm sure."

"Have you ever hurt her?"

"No," he says. "I'm not . . . I don't do that. I mean, I've . . . I've definitely hurt her feelings and . . . I'm sure I've hurt her in little ways, but . . . not in the way you mean."

"Have you ever hit her?"

"No."

I don't need the VSA to tell me he's lying.

I narrow my gaze at him and lock my eyes onto his.

He looks away.

"I've never punched her or beat her up or anything like that," he says. "I've . . . There have been times when she went crazy and I've had to subdue her. I may have slapped her or . . . but never hit or punched or anything like that. We'd get into arguments sometimes. She'd lose it and freak the fuck out. She'd scream at me, throw things at me, hit me. Hit me over and over. I never hit her back. But I'd grab her and stop her from hitting me.

Hold her until she calmed down. She said I hurt her some of those times."

"So your answer to my question have you ever hurt her should've been yes."

"I guess so. Technically. But not to the way you mean it. She's not missing 'cause I hurt her."

"If everything you've told us is true, and I'm not convinced it is, she is missing because you left her alone, stranded on the river."

"I . . . I shouldn't've done that. But you don't know how she could get. And I tried to get her to let me take her back to the landing, but she wouldn't let me. You want to blame me for what happened, but what about blaming her? She's the one who refused to get in the boat. She's the one who chose to stay out there."

"What reasons did she give you for not wanting to leave with you?" I ask.

"Said she wasn't ready to leave, that she didn't want to go back yet. Said she knew I was just going to drop her off and head back out there without her."

"Were you?"

He nods. "Probably."

"Why?"

"I had just had enough of her bullshit."

"What else did she say?"

"That . . . that I had just taken her out there to fuck her, and once I had done that I was ready to take her back, that I was treating her like a whore."

"Is that true?"

"Not the whore part, but . . . I thought that's what we went out there to do. I didn't know she wanted to . . . talk and hang out and shit."

"So if you had just stayed a little longer . . . everything would've been fine and she would've gone back with you later?"

He shrugs. "There was never any predicting her moods."

"Did you go straight back to the landing?" I ask.

"Yes."

"What'd you do then?"

"Loaded up the boat and—"

"Anyone see you?"

He looks up, squinting. "Yeah, there was . . . There were two girls in a car turning around. I waved to them. Didn't recognize them."

"We'll need a full description of them and their vehicle."

"Okay. I noticed they had a Georgia tag."

"Then what'd you do?"

"Went straight home and climbed into bed."

"Anyone see you?" I ask. "Anyone able to verify what you're saying?"

He shrugs. "I'm sure Mom saw my truck in the driveway if she looked out—and she usually does."

"Usually does what?"

"Looks out. Knows when I come and go."

"Who do you think the other footprints at your camp belong to?"

He shrugs.

"Probably whoever picked her up."

"You say *her* a lot," I say. "Is there a reason you don't want to say her name?"

"No."

"When's the last time you were out at your cabin before you and Carla were there?" I ask.

He shrugs.

"That won't do," I say. "The only way out of this is for you to tell the truth—no matter what it is. You know when you were out there last."

"Earlier today," he says as if it gives him physical pain to do so. "Or yesterday, whatever it is. What time is it?"

"You were out at your camp earlier on Sunday before you went back out there with Carla?"

He nods.

"I need a verbal response."

"Yeah."

"Who was with you?" I ask.

He doesn't respond for a moment, then says, "Cindy."

"Cindy Capps?" I ask.

"Yeah."

Cindy Denise Capps, or CDC as she is known to many, is our town's only official sex worker.

"You took her out to your cabin to have sex with earlier in the day?" I ask.

"Yeah."

"Did Carla figure it out?" I ask. "Is that what upset her?"

"She said the cabin smelled like sex, and she found one of Cindy's cigarette butts."

CHAPTER
NINETEEN

CDC LIVES in one of the old redbrick government housing units across from the high school football field.

I knock on her door at a little before six.

When she opens the door she says, "Hey, John."

She's a pale, voluptuous, thirty-something white woman with green eyes and an auburn tint to her dark hair. Flecks of mascara cling to her eyelashes, and each of her nails has a little glitter-blue polish remnant on it.

"Sorry to show up so early," I say.

"You caught me just in time. Was just about to head to bed."

She's in a too-short Freewheelin' Bob Dylan t-shirt—and based on the pubic hair peeking out beneath it and the nipples of her enormous breasts poking out near the top of it that's all she's in.

"Glad I did," I say.

"This must be official business," she says. "Can't remember the last time you showed up here empty handed."

Except for on a few rare occasions I've only showed up at Cindy's door to deliver food or medicine or clothes—and when it comes to this last I make a mental note to bring longer t-shirts in the future. She knows I'm not here to arrest her. I'd never arrest a sex worker. A sex trafficker or a john using an underage girl, yes, but never a sex worker, and she knows it.

"Sorry about that," I say. "Been out all night searching for Carla. Came straight here from the sheriff's office."

"Carla missin'?"

"Yeah. You seen her or heard anything?"

She shakes her head. "But I'll let you know if I do."

"Thanks. Just got a quick question for you and I'll let you get to bed."

"Fire away."

"Mason Hayes," I say. "Did you go to his river camp with him yesterday?"

She shakes her head. "He's come by here for a piece of pussy now and then over the years, but not in a while. I've never gone anywhere with him. Is he in the jail?"

"Yeah. Why?"

"I had a collect call from an inmate in the Gulf County jail a little while ago, but I didn't accept it."

"He was probably calling to tell you he'd pay you to back his lie," I say.

She nods. "Probably so."

"If he calls back, would you accept it and let me know what he says? I'll pay the charges."

"'Course."

"Thanks."

"Hope you find Carla soon," she says. "Hope she's okay. For what it's worth . . . I know a little about men, and I can't see Mason hurting or killing a woman. He's not the type. I know the type. And he ain't it."

As I'm driving back to the sheriff's office, Dad calls.

"Merrill told me about Carla," he says. "What can I do?"

"Can't think of anything at the moment," I say.

"I hope she's just . . . and will turn up soon. Anything you need, just let me know. I'll call Fred and let him know that the resources of my office are at your disposal."

"Thanks."

"I know what she means to you, what you mean to her," he says. "How are you holding up?"

"Trying not to think too much about . . . Just workin the case —like it's any other case."

"Let me know what I can do for you, how I can help you."

I swallow hard against the lump in my throat and say, "Thanks."

"Merrill asked for time off to help with the search," he says. "I denied the request. He can help you in any way you need, but I don't want him having to use his vacation time. He can stay on the clock and be a loan from this office."

"Thank you," I say. "I really—"

"Just let me know if there's anything else I can do."

CHAPTER
TWENTY

"YOU SHOULD'VE CALLED ME," Fred Miller is saying.

I'm seated in a chair across from his desk—a monstrosity of solid cherry wood with an elegant and elaborate matching cherry wood nameplate with "Sheriff Fred Miller" in big, boxy bold letters. The only other objects on the desk are a phone, a calendar, and a six shooter cylinder pen holder, all of which look lost on the large open surface of the desk.

He's sipping hot coffee from a large paper cup, the steam of which curls up and around his nose each time he drinks.

"Wasn't sure what we had," I say. "Still not. I'm hoping she's gonna drive up this morning wondering what all the fuss is about."

He nods. "I hope that happens. I really do. But you were right to handle it the way you did—apart from not calling me. I'd rather waste time, money, and manpower searching for someone who was never really missing than get a late start searching for someone who is."

"I appreciate that."

The walls of his office are decorated with large-framed Old West and cowboy prints of the bright, vivid, romanticized, mass-produced variety.

Though there are no traces of Reggie remaining in his office, I will always think of it as hers, and it makes me uncomfortable to be in it. And it doesn't matter that it has been well over a year since she died or that she never felt like it was hers anyway.

As if sensing my unease and ever the politician, he says, "I've been thinking we need to create some sort of memorial to Sheriff Summers somewhere in the office. Only female sheriff in our county's history. Only sheriff killed in the line of duty. You knew her the best and . . . I know y'all were close. When you can, be thinking of what you feel would be appropriate and let's work on it together."

I nod. "I will. Thanks."

"Okay, so tell me what we've got," he says.

I do.

"Well, hopefully the arson investigator and the FDLE crime scene techs will be able to tell us more this morning."

I nod.

"Strange that her car is gone," he says. "Hopefully, she just wanted to get away and will turn up this morning like you said. Don't want you feelin' like a fool if she does."

"I won't," I say. "I'd do it all over again."

"Good."

We are quiet for a moment.

"Will's a good man and a great dentist. I hope his little shit of a son didn't do anything . . . stupid. Let's see what the VSA says about what he's saying."

"I've already caught him in one big lie," I say.

"What's that?"

I tell him.

"Wonder why he'd lie about who he was out there with before Carla? Shouldn't have any bearing on what happened later with her."

"It could mean that it does," I say. "Or he could be embarrassed or . . . I plan to confront him with it and the results of the VSA this morning."

He nods. "You get any sleep yet?"

"Not yet," I say.

"Well, go get some. We've got plenty of good people working on this now."

"I will," I lie.

CHAPTER
TWENTY-ONE

"YOU LIED TO ME," I say to Mason.

I have him back in the interview room, recording what he says.

He frowns and nods.

"Why?"

He shrugs.

I don't say what he lied to me about. I want him to tell me that. According to the VSA, he lied about a lot.

"Why lie?" I ask.

He shakes his head slowly, seemingly in shame.

"Guilty people lie," I say.

He nods.

"Mostly to cover up their crimes."

"I ain't committed no crimes," he says. "Already told you that."

"Then why lie?"

He shrugs again. "I don't know. It was stupid. I was . . . embarrassed. Thought it'd look bad."

"Thought what would look bad?"

"Who I was out there with that afternoon," he says.

"Which wasn't Cindy."

"No, it wasn't. I just said CDC 'cause I thought . . ."

"You thought you could call her before I talked to her and pay her to lie for you, but why? Why do you need an alibi for yesterday afternoon?"

"I don't. Not an alibi. I just . . . didn't want to say who I was with."

"Why?"

"Why do I even have to say? The afternoon has nothing to do with Carla, right? So . . . I think . . . I'm not gonna answer any more questions, and I want a lawyer."

I nod. "Okay."

I pull out my phone, call his dad, place the phone on the table between us, and put it on speaker.

"John," Will says. "Have you found her? Please tell me she turned up on her own and is all good."

"No, not yet," I say.

"Damn it. I was hoping . . ."

"Will, I've got you on speaker," I say. "I'm here with Mason. He's been lying to me and now he's refusing to answer any more questions and is asking for an attorney."

"Dad," Mason says, "I didn't have anything to do with Carla goin' missin'. I ain't lyin' about that. I swear."

"Why are you lyin' about anything?" Will says. "Where did I go wrong with you, boy?"

"I'm just . . . I haven't committed any crimes. I ain't done nothin' wrong . . . as far as the law is concerned."

"Then tell John what it is."

"It's personal," he says. "Private."

"Nothing is right now," I say. "Not until we find Carla."

"John," Will says. "I believe him. I don't think he has broken any laws or hurt Carla, but I do think he needs a lawyer. If it was just you . . . but I don't trust everybody in the sheriff's department like I do you."

"I understand," I say.

"But, Mason . . ." Will says, "if you didn't do anything illegal and having nothing to do with Carla's disappearance . . . I want you to cooperate fully with John. Answer his questions truthfully right now or I'm cutting you off, taking back your house and truck and boat, and you can go get a real job."

"Okay, okay. I will. It's just . . . I . . . I was . . . I took Lily to the cabin yesterday afternoon."

"Who?" I ask.

Will says, "His married ex-girlfriend. Lilian Battle. Well, Lillian Mosely now. When did you start seein' her again?"

"I . . . ain't really seein' her."

"Just having sex with her in my cabin," Will says.

"I . . . We . . . It just happened."

"It didn't just happen," Will says. "And I bet that wasn't the first time it happened, was it?"

"It was stupid, and I'm sorry, daddy. I am, but . . . it has nothin' to do with Carla bein' missin'. I had nothing to do with that."

"If you called her and asked her to lie for you, we'll have a record of it," I say. "And if you did it from in here we'll have a recording."

"I haven't called her. I didn't ask her to lie for me. I swear."

Will says, "I thought by loving you and giving you every advantage and opportunity you'd grow up to be a good man, do something with your life, but you're just a . . ."

Mason opens his mouth to say something, but nothing comes out. Will continues.

"John, I'm sorry about all this. I am. I feel like a lot of it is my fault. I don't think he had anything to do with Carla disappearing—besides leaving her out there—but I find all his other actions abhorrent."

"I was stupid," Mason says. "And I'm sorry, but I didn't do anything to Carla. I was home in bed. Ask Mom."

Will says, "John, you don't have to take Beth's word for it, though I would hope you would. We have a security system at our place. It will show when he left and when he came home."

CHAPTER
TWENTY-TWO

LILIAN MOSELY IS A SWEET, vivacious, fresh-faced kindergarten teacher whose students and their parents adore her. She's a late twenties white woman with thick brown hair pulled up in a ponytail and big, bright brown eyes. Not quite five and half feet tall, she has a certain softness bordering on fluffiness to her that gives her the hint of matronliness, though in the most positive sense of that word.

Her classroom is cluttered with a variety of art projects in various stages of completion and smells of popcorn, glue, and sweaty children.

Each tiny desk has the alphabet, the student's name, a bottle of water, and a plastic token holder held in place by velcro.

The letter for today is E, which is written on the chalkboard with several words that begin with it and an accompanying drawing, and on the desks are construction paper elephant hats with ribbon trunks hanging down in the front.

The classroom is empty apart from me and Lily. We have a few uninterrupted, private minutes before her students return from PE.

She acts nervous and fidgety and is beginning to perspire.

"Is everything okay?" she asks. "Did something happen to Joel?"

Joel Mosely, who works for the electrical co-op, is her husband.

"No, he's fine," I say. "Carla Pearson is missing."

"Carla? Really? Wow. I'm sorry to—"

I can see her make the connection between Carla and Mason and Mason and her.

"I'm trying to find her," I say. "She went on the river with Mason Hayes yesterday evening. It's the last anyone has seen of her."

"Is Mason missing too?"

"No."

"Okay, well, I haven't seen her. I don't really know Carla all that well, but if I see or a hear anything I'll—"

"Mason said you and he went to his family's cabin yesterday afternoon," I say.

Her body seems to collapse in on itself a little, and she closes her eyes and frowns.

When she opens her eyes, there are tears in them.

"I . . . What does that have to do with—"

"Did you go to the cabin with him?"

She swallows hard and then slowly nods. "I regretted doing it before I did it. I've been eaten up with guilt. It was . . . the worst most stupid thing I have ever done. Joel is a good guy. He is. He doesn't deserve to be . . . to have me . . . I've never . . . I don't have an excuse. Can't even tell you why I did it. God, if this gets out . . ."

"Have you been seeing Mason?" I ask.

She shakes her head. "No. He's an old boyfriend. I've been . . . I've been feeling . . . fat and just sort of . . . lost . . . and when he showed me some attention . . . He broke up with me back when we were . . . and I guess I always felt . . . I don't know, kind of rejected and . . . hurt, so when he showed interest in me now with how I'm lookin' and feelin' . . . I fell into a . . . I can't believe how stupid and pathetic it was. And now this. Oh my God. My life is over."

I shake my head. "It's not. I'm not here to do you any harm. I'm just trying to get the truth out of Mason."

"Well, he's tellin' the truth if he said the stupidest girl in the world went to his cabin with him."

"What time did y'all go?" I ask. "How long did you stay? What time did you get back?"

"Mid-afternoon," she says. "Maybe three. I . . . We weren't there long. Just long enough for me to make the biggest mistake of my life. Back before four. We went our separate ways, and I haven't seen or spoken to him since."

"How'd he seem?"

"Fine. His usual self. Not . . . He didn't seem like he'd . . . that he could hurt anyone or anything like that."

"Did you see Carla or anyone else on the river or at the camp or the landing?"

She shakes her head. "I had a big floppy hat, big sunshades, and a big raincoat. I didn't want to be seen, and I was looking down mostly, trying to hide my face."

"Did Mason say or do anything off, odd, or suspicious?"

"Not at all. We didn't talk much. But he was his normal self. I feel so ashamed. Who else knows?"

"Only his dad as far as I know."

"Oh my God, Dr. Hayes knows. I . . . can't . . . I'm gonna have to get a new dentist. I can never face him again. I know I don't deserve it, but can you please, please not tell anyone else? It's not even for me as much as Joel. It would destroy him."

"Any chance Joel knows or followed you or Mason or—"

"No. He was playing golf in Dothan with his buddies."

"Did you follow Mason or Carla or go back out to the cabin last night?"

"No," she says. "Of course not. I . . . Why would you even ask me something like—"

"I have to ask," I say. "And I'm wondering why with the rain and other people walking up and down the path later why your footprints would still be out there."

CHAPTER
TWENTY-THREE

"THIS WASN'T the result of a lighting strike," Vic Roberts is saying.

I am back out at the McDaniel's camp with our district's lead arson investigator.

He's a short African-American man with a receding hairline that makes a kind of half-moon on the front part of his head. His glasses always seem so smudged and smeared I wonder how he sees out of them.

"What we have here is a deliberately set fire."

He points down at the spot where the fire had been.

Everything has been removed except for the wooden tabletop.

"We've bagged all the materials in the fire and will take them to the lab,"

"Look at that burn pattern," he says, pointing at the charred spot on the tabletop. "See that characteristic crocodile skin look?"

I nod.

"That's where your deepest char is," he says. "Your point of origin. And we've detected the use of an accelerant. We're gonna cut out this section of the table and transport it to the lab.

The center here where the fire was hottest will have consumed all the accelerant used, but here on the edges we should be able to recover some and hopefully identify it. I'd say the fire got away from the arsonist. See the burn marks shooting up the walls."

I glance around. There are no gas cans or lighter fluid containers about. "Any accelerants been discovered?"

He shakes his head and pushes his glasses back up on his nose.

"So whoever started it took whatever he or she used," I say. "And probably brought it to begin with. What was in the fire?"

"A lot of limbs and wood, leaves and trash from dry spots inside the cabin," he says, "but the interesting items are what looks to be newer clothes—not like the old and faded and weathered materials from inside here."

Though I was expecting this, my stomach drops at the possibility of Carla's clothes being burned to hide evidence, and I feel dizzy and lightheaded.

"Most of it was destroyed," he says, "but we'll recover and identify what we can in the lab. Thing is . . . there were plenty more old dry materials to provide fuel for the fire. There was no need to destroy new clothes. If the fire was for warmth or to keep out animals or to cook over, we'd expect only the older materials used, but because there is new clothing . . . It was most likely set for the purpose of destroying evidence."

I nod and take several deep breaths.

"The chair is . . . odd," he says, his forehead furrowing just beneath the half-moon of his head. "What we have to ask is . . . is there any natural means of heat transfer from the closet to the fire on the chair? Or are there any natural means of heat transfer from the fire on the chair to the closet?"

"Which is it?" I ask.

"Neither," he says. "Appears to be the third option. Two different fires. We can find no means of communication between the two fires."

"Find any remnants of anything that was burned on the chair?" I ask.

He shakes his head. "We'll run tests at the lab, but there's nothing visible."

"Any theories?" I ask.

"Most household materials like the padding on the chair are made with flame retardant chemicals these days. They could've tried to burn something on the chair but couldn't get a good enough fire going, so they dragged the table over partially into the closet and started over. They got it going good in there. Got away from them. But that's just a theory. No way to know for certain, but hopefully we'll know more once we get everything back to the lab and run some tests. I'll let you know."

CHAPTER
TWENTY-FOUR

SEARCH AND RESCUE boats are trolling up and down the river. Deputies, wildlife officers, and volunteers are scouring the swamps. FDLE's crime scene unit is processing the Hayes and McDaniel cabins.

Michelle, who is coordinating with FDLE, meets me at the Hayes's dock.

She hands me a clear plastic evidence bag with a padlock in it. The lock is a medium-sized Master Magnum Heavy-Duty padlock with a black body and silver shackle. It's locked and there's no key with it.

"CSI found this on the north side of the cabin in the swamp," she says. "Just like this—locked with no key. It looks pretty new, doesn't it? Definitely in good condition. Don't think it's been out there long. There's a storage box with the hasp partially ripped off of it on the porch. Figure it goes to it. Looks like it was just thrown into the swamp—probably from the porch."

I nod.

"Have you slept yet?"

I shake my head.

"You need to. Have you eaten?"

As she asks that, I realize I haven't been drinking anything either.

I'm exhausted, hungry, and dehydrated, and all I want to do is get into the swamp and search for Carla.

"Go home," she says. "Get some sleep. Eat something. Get a shower. Then come back."

"I can't."

A new boatload of volunteers arrives and ties up at the dock. Among them is Charlene Childs, a civic-minded woman in her early forties who is somehow related to Lawton Childs, the former Florida Governor who served two terms from 1990-1998.

As the others are led to the back of the cabin to join the search teams, Charlene walks over to me and Michelle.

"Are you okay?" she asks. "You don't look so good."

"Just a little tired."

She says, "Go get some rest. We have some great volunteers. We'll find her. And for the record, I've known Mason since he was a little boy. He's a very sweet boy. No way he had anything to do with Carla's disappearance. He should've never left her out here, but . . ."

I nod. "Thank you for helping."

She nods toward her boat. "There's cold water and some food in there. And the benches are covered. Why don't you eat and drink something and lay down for a few minutes. Join us when you get to feeling better?"

Michelle says, "That's exactly what you're going to do."

As Charlene walks toward the back of the cabin and Michelle rejoins FDLE, I climb down into the boat, drink two bottles of water, and lie down on one of the padded benches in the shade.

I'm asleep in seconds.

And then the dreams come.

The last of the setting sun streaks the blue horizon with neon pink and splatters the emerald green waters of the Gulf with giant orange splotches like scoops of sherbet in an Art Deco bowl.

A fitting finale for a perfect Florida day.

My son, who looks to be around four—though it's hard to tell since in dreams we all seem ageless—runs up from the water's edge, his face red with sun and heat, his hands sticky with wet sand, and asks me to join him for one last swim.

Though my son looks a bit like John Paul and a bit like Nash, he is neither.

He looks up at me with his mother's brown eyes, as open and honest as possible, and smiles his sweetest smile as he begins to beg.

"Please, Daddy," he says. "Please."

"We need to go," I say. "It'll be dark soon. And I'm supposed to take your mom out on a date tonight."

"Please, Daddy," he repeats as if I have not spoken, and now he takes the edge of my swimming trunks in his tiny, sandy hand and tugs.

I look down at him, moved by his openness, purity, and beauty.

He knows he's got me then.

"Yes," he says, releasing my shorts to clench his fist and pull it toward him in a gesture of victory. Then he begins to jump up and down.

I drop the keys and the towels and the bottles of sunscreen wrapped in them, kick off my flip-flops, and pause just a moment to take it all in—him, the sand, the sea, the sun.

"I love you, Dad," he says with the ease and unashamed openness only a safe and secure child can.

"I love you."

I take his hand in mine, and we walk down to the end of his world as the sun sets and the breeze cools off the day. And we walk right into the ocean from which we came. A wave knocks us down and we stay that way, allowing the foamy water to wash over us.

He shrieks his joy and excitement, sounding like the gulls in the air and on the shore. He plays with intensity and abandon, and for a moment I want to be a child again, but only for a moment, for more than anything in this world, I want to be his dad.

We forget about the world around us, and we lose track of time, and the thick, salty waters of the Gulf roll in on us and then back out to sea.

When we walk back up onto the beach, Carla is there waiting for us.

"Why didn't you bring John Paul?" she asks.

I have no answer.

"I thought you'd be more of a father to him. You're so good with your girls . . . and Nash. Why don't you do more for John Paul? Will you do more if I leave?"

"Where are you going?" I ask. "Don't go."

"It's not my choice, John."

"Please stay. He needs you. Please don't go."

"Goodbye, John. Thanks for all you did for me. You were my . . . You were the only one I could ever really count on."

She walks down into the water and keeps walking.

I am unable to move, unable to stop her, powerless to do anything but stand there and watch as she vanishes into the now-dark waters of the Gulf.

I startle awake and sit up feeling worse than when I had laid down.

My heart is racing, and I'm filled with a deep, dark sense of dread.

Fred Miller is standing with Michelle on the dock, and the feeling of embarrassment joins everything else I'm feeling.

I grab another bottle of water, poor some into my hands, splash my face with it, drink the rest, then join them on the dock.

"I told you to go home and get some sleep," Miller says. "We've got a small army of people out here looking for her. You go get some proper rest and then come back."

"Is FDLE finished?" I ask.

Michelle nods. "No signs of violence in the cabin. They lifted more prints, but that's about it. We need to get the shoes Mason and Lily were wearing so we can match them."

I nod. "I'll—"

"You'll go home," Miller says.

"Okay," I say, "but let me get Lillian Mosley's shoes on the way. I told her we'd try to keep her name out of this and—"

"Unless she had something to do with it," he says.

"Of course," I say. "But until we have any evidence at all that she might have . . . I'd like for as few people to know about her as possible."

"Fine," he says. "You're a hell of a detective, but sometimes you can tell you used to be a chaplain."

CHAPTER
TWENTY-FIVE

"I WISH you'd sleep some more," Anna is saying.

I squint up at her.

She is seated on the edge of our bed.

Though I had set an alarm, I asked her to make sure I was up in case I slept through it.

It had taken a while to get off the river and go by and get Mason and Lillian's shoes, and I haven't been in bed long. My eyes and head are hurting, and I feel groggy and out of it.

Anna is dressed casually. Her hair is down. She has no makeup on, which makes her look younger, her features softer, and I'm overcome by a desire to pull her into bed with me.

"You are so beautiful," I say.

Reaching up, I gently touch her cheek. She turns her head into my hand and kisses it.

I push myself up and lean against the wall.

She hands me a large Los Angeles Lakers Tervis Tumbler full of cold coffee.

I take a big gulp and say, "Thanks."

"How are you?" I ask. "How are the kids?"

"How are *you*?" she asks.

I shake my head. "I can't . . . lose her."

She nods.

"But," I add, "every passing minute . . . makes it less likely that we'll find her alive. How is John Paul doing?"

"He's okay. Been asking about his mom some, but mostly he's good. He really wanted her when it was bedtime last night. That seems to be the time he misses her most."

"Sorry I wasn't here to help with him last night."

"Don't worry about anything here," she says. "I got this. We're all good. Just do what you need to to find her. Anything I can do to help you?"

Before I can tell her there's not, Taylor and John Paul open the bedroom door and rush into the room. As is their custom, they climb onto the bed and begin jumping. As is my custom, I begin to tussle with and tickle and hug them—doing the last even more intensely than usual if possible.

Eventually Taylor and John Paul grow bored wrestling with me and wander out of our bedroom in search of fun elsewhere.

I lift my phone from the bedside table and look at it.

I've missed several calls and have several unread text messages.

The two that I go to first are from Sam Michaels and Merrick McKnight.

Sam is an FDLE agent. I've worked with her and her husband, Daniel, on several cases over the years. Merrick is a journalist and had been Reggie's significant other for several years.

Anna says, "Sam called me when she couldn't get you. Said she and Daniel are eager to help in any way they can. Just let them know what they can do."

I listen to Sam's message, which reiterates what Anna just shared with me.

Merrick didn't leave a message, just a text that reads: Heard about Carla. Call me if I can help in any way.

"Means a lot that they reached out," I say.

"Means even more that they mean it," she says. "You've helped each of them in so many ways over the years. They'd do anything for you. Let them help if there's something they can do."

CHAPTER
TWENTY-SIX

IT'S GETTING dark by the time I'm climbing back into my truck.

Since it's too dark to search the river or the swamp, I decide to interview some of the people Carla has been hanging out with lately. I don't refer to them as her friends because I don't think they are.

I start with Bailey Bozeman.

I find her hanging out in front of the laundromat, drinking a beer and smoking a cigarette in the parking lot near her car while waiting for her clothes.

The laundromat is inside part of an old convenience store building on Highway 22 not far from our house. A yet-to-open game room is in the other part. Contrasting the unlit parking lot, it's bright inside the washateria where an enormous Samoan-looking man dozes in the blue plastic chair his girth eclipses. Only two of the large industrial dryers are in use, their contents tumbling slowly around.

"John fuckin' Jordan," she says. "Here to arrest me for loitering?"

I'm surprised she knows that word, but I suspect when she

was younger she has been accused of that very thing and asked to leave.

She's a large, loud, irreverent, often-obnoxious young woman with thick curly blond hair and lots and lots of it. The other thing she has lots and lot of is ink—including full sleeves on both her arms, a neck and chin tattoo.

She is backlit by the laundromat, which adds to the dramatic nature of her appearance.

"Still looking for Carla," I say.

"That hooker hasn't shown up yet? She must be havin' a hell of a good time."

"I don't think so."

"You worry too much," she says.

"I'm tellin' you she's with her new dude laid up somewhere."

"Her new dude is laid up in the Gulf County jail," I say.

"*Whaaa*?" she says, raising the pitch of her voice and holding it out. "For what? You think his bitch ass did somethin' to your girl?"

"Is he capable?"

"We're all capable. But . . . I can't see it. Mason's a whiny little bitch still suckin' on his mama's fake tit. He's weak. Livin' off his daddy's money."

She finishes her cigarette and immediately lights another, then takes a long draw on it like she hasn't had one in forever.

All her movements have a shaky, frenetic quality to them, as if she's on something or needs to be.

"If she's not with Mason, any idea where she might be?"

"Not the faintest."

It makes me sad for Carla that Bailey is what passes for a friend—someone who is so damaged, so wounded, so altered by drugs and alcohol that she can't care for herself, let alone someone else.

"I reached out to everyone you said she had been hanging out with lately. No one responded or returned my calls."

"Everybody's busy. You know how it is. Plus, nobody gonna call a cop back."

"Would you mind reaching out to them to see if they have any ideas about where she might be?"

"Sure," she says. "Just give me some pig pay or a Get Out Of Jail Free card."

"Got no Get Out Of Jail Free cards, but you help me with this and I won't forget it if you ever get into a jam in the future."

"It's not if but when," she says.

"Well, whenever that is . . . I'll do what I can."

"I'll make some calls."

"Why did you include her ex-boyfriend on the list?" I ask.

"Whatcha mean?"

"Has she seen him lately?"

"*Yeah,*" she says, like it's obvious and I was stupid to ask it.

"Where?"

"Whatcha mean *where*? They didn't run into each other at the Dollar Store or some shit like that. They sneak off and fuck. Don't think they ever stopped. If they did it wasn't for long."

"She's been seeing Mason and Easton?"

She nods.

"Did Mason know?"

She shrugs. "Don't think so."

"What about Easton's wife?"

CHAPTER
TWENTY-SEVEN

I CALL Easton Stevens again as I pull out of the laundromat onto 22.

Like the times before, it goes straight to his voicemail.

"Easton," I say after the beep, "it's John Jordan. It's very important that I speak with you. I'm looking for Carla Pearson. I've called you several times. Left several messages. I'm on my way to your house now. If you don't want me to ask my questions in front of your wife, call me back and tell me where we can meet."

As soon as I end the call, I click on the little blue cartoon bubble and text him a similar message.

He calls me back within minutes.

"Don't come to my house," he says. "I'll meet you."

"Where?"

"I don't want to be seen with you," he says. "How about T.L. James?"

"On my way," I say.

Easton and Meg Stevens live in Whispering Pines, a subdivision started in the late 70s or early 80s not far from T.L. James Park. Their home, which they inherited from Meg's mom, stands on a large lot among tall, thick, old-growth pine trees.

T.L. James Park is a sports complex with four softball fields, basketball and tennis courts, a small youth football field, a horse arena, picnic tables, and a playground.

The park is so close to his home I figure he's going to walk to it—which is confirmed when I arrive and don't see his vehicle.

I pull down the narrow asphalt drive between the sparse row of planted palms, pass the horse arena and the football field, continue onto the grass parking lot, park, and get out.

I walk past the tennis courts and find him sitting on top of a blue mesh picnic table beneath the first pavilion.

The pavilion is low, and I have to duck a little to walk under it. He's sitting on the top of the table with his feet on the bench. He's nervous and looks paranoid.

"I only have a minute," he says. "Told Meg I wanted some fresh air. She's gonna be suspicious. I never go out walking. Never go out for fresh air."

"Surely she won't think you're calling or meeting another woman."

He resembles Mason enough to make me think Carla has a type. He's older, thicker, more filled out, his hair is shorter, and he's less privileged and polished. Unlike Mason, being country or redneck is not a choice, not an affect.

"Got no idea where Carla is," he says. "I would've called you back if I did."

"When's the last time you saw her?" I ask.

He shrugs. "Not sure. Been a while."

"I understand you two are still seeing each other."

"What? *No.* Who said that?"

I can tell he's lying.

He sits up some and looks anxiously over my shoulder. I turn and follow his gaze. In the far distance, two boys arrive on bicycles with a basketball and begin to shoot on the goals. Merrill and I have played on the goals several times over the years when the old gym has been closed for repairs.

"It's just kids hoopin'," I say. "They can barely see each other, let alone us, but we can get in my truck and go for a ride if you'd like to get away from here."

He shakes his head. "No. Just hurry with your questions."

"I'm not going to hurry," I say. "And I'm not going to accept lies. Someone I care about very deeply is missing—someone you once cared about. Now, I'm tryin' to accommodate your desire for discretion, though I don't like aiding your deceit, but I can go over to your house and do this in front of your wife or I can take you to the sheriff's office or you can start cooperating here and now. Your choice."

"I do care about her," he says. "I . . . But I don't know where she is."

"I asked when the last time you saw her was, and you avoided the question," I say. "I asked if y'all have been seeing each other, and you lied to me."

"I didn't lie."

"Y'all haven't continued to see each other?" I ask.

"I just meant . . . the last time was the last time. I couldn't risk . . . If something like that gets out, it'll mean the end of my marriage. Meg is very jealous and paranoid."

"Can't imagine why," I say. "Are you seeing any other women or just Carla?"

"I ain't *seein'* Carla. Quit sayin' that."

"Easton," I say. "This is serious. It's an official missing persons case. And it isn't just anyone. It's Carla. You don't get to lie and get away with it. Not now."

"I . . . I'm . . . Can you keep it between us? It would destroy Meg and . . ."

"If it has no bearing on her disappearance, I'll do everything I can to keep it quiet. What else were you going to say?"

"We just found out . . ."

"Found out what?"

"That . . . Meg is pregnant. I don't want her hearing anything that would upset her."

"Did you tell Carla?"

"*What*? No. But it was the last time. I swear it. Carla and I don't work—not as a couple, but . . . she . . . We . . . There's this thing between us. Like a pull, you know? We're so . . . I'm so attracted to her. I've tried to stop but . . ."

"But you just can't quit her," I say.

"Yeah," he says, without any indication he gets the reference.

"When's the last time you were with her?" I ask.

He hesitates. "Yesterday."

"When?"

"Yesterday morning . . . while Meg was at church."

"Where?"

"She parked her car at Iola Landing and got in the truck with me. We rode around for a while, found a place to park, and . . . I told her it was the last time. I swear I did. We both knew how wrong it was. Felt so bad about it, but . . . She's a better person than me. I'd see her any chance I got, but she'd only see me when she and Mason weren't together. They've been breaking up and getting back together a lot lately."

"Did anyone see you two together?"

He shakes his head. "I don't think so."

"Who all knew about y'all?"

"Didn't think anybody did."

"Did y'all argue?"

"No. I swear. Everything was . . . She was fine when I dropped her off at her car. I swear it on my life."

"Did she say that was the last time or did you?"

"We both did. We've been sayin' it a while. Just haven't been able to do it yet. But we meant it. It wasn't . . . We weren't upset. Just sort of sad."

"Any ideas where she could be?"

"She's been seein' Mason Hayes some. Might be with him."

"She's not."

He shrugs. "I don't know. She usually doesn't go far from her kid. She's a good mom. Says she learned most of what she knows about parenting from you and Anna."

"She been upset about anything lately? Worried? Mention anyone bothering her?"

"I'm gonna be honest with you, John. I . . . I know you don't want to hear this, and I don't want to be saying it, but the truth is . . . we didn't talk a lot. We just didn't. Even when we were a couple."

"If you hear anything or think of anything else, call me as soon as possible," I say. "And if I find out you've lied to me . . ."

"I haven't," he says. "I swear. I hope you find her soon and she's okay. I do care for her. She's a . . . she's a very good person. Thinks the sun rises and sets with you."

CHAPTER
TWENTY-EIGHT

HOW COULD I have failed Carla so completely?

How could she be seeing either one of these guys, let alone both of them?

Each in their own way, each of them in virtually every way, is unworthy of her. They aren't her intellectual or emotional equals. They are immature, self-centered boys still refusing to grow up.

It's obvious neither of them treated her well, neither of them treated her like she deserved.

I always knew that given the fact that her father was alcoholic and absentee, Carla was likely to subconsciously date a string of losers to recreate the dynamic she had with her dad, but foolishly I thought I could change that.

Until recently I had thought that my presence in her life, the way I cared for and treated her, the way she witnessed me care for Anna and Johanna and Taylor and even Susan, would cause her to refuse to settle for someone who treated her like her biological father had and still does.

The sheriff's comment about me at times still acting like a chaplain instead of a detective reverberates through my head. But what he doesn't get is that I've never been one or the other, never acted like one instead of the other. I am both. My time as a chaplain seems like a lifetime ago now, and even back then I was as much an investigator as I was a minister. But he's right—I do take a certain spiritual social worker approach to my work as a detective. And since leaving chaplaincy my work as a kind of minister counselor has found an outlet in helping and taking care of people like Carla and John Paul.

In moments like these, I feel like I've failed—failed as a minister and counselor and surrogate father.

I thought I was making a difference. I was delusional.

The fact that she has been involved with young men like Easton and Mason shows her lack of self-esteem, self-care, and self-regard. It shows that in spite of everything or because of it, she is still an insecure little girl looking for her daddy's love and approval.

And the fact that she's seeing both of these self-centered boys simultaneously shows just how deeply that insecurity goes.

I have fooled myself that I was making a difference in her life —or at least about the degree to which I was making a difference or the kind of difference I have been making. Here is yet another example of the absurdity and futility of my savior complex.

What else could I have done?

Should I have tried to get her away from Rudy when she was younger? I couldn't have adopted her. I was a single man living in a dilapidated single-wide trailer at the time.

I still vividly remember the night that Nicole Caldwell was murdered in my office at PCI.

When I arrived at Rudy's just before three in the morning, I drained the remainder of my bottle and threw it toward the dumpster. Careening off the side, the bottle hit the powdered oyster shell parking lot and shot up a small puff of white dust.

I sprayed my mouth with breath freshener and opened the door to the diner quietly, hoping not to wake Carla, who was slumped on a barstool, her head resting on her outstretched arm next to open school books on the counter.

My coordination wasn't as trustworthy as it usually was, and I was unable to prevent the cowbell above the door from clanging.

She bolted upright and spun around toward me.

Her blond hair was mussed and stuck out on one side, her brilliant green eyes soft and moist, their confused, sleepy quality only adding to her vulnerability.

"I tried to wait up for you," she said. "I heard what happened. Are you okay?"

I wondered if she was referring to the Billy Ray Dickens attempted escape or if word of Nicole's death had already spread through town.

At just seventeen, Carla had the old soul of a motherless daughter trapped in a small town with an alcoholic father and had a tendency toward care-taking.

"Can I have some coffee?" I asked as I made my way to my booth in the back.

"Sure," she said, studying me for a moment before adding, "I'll bring the pot."

I made it to the booth and pitched into it.

The thick smell of old grease and stale cigarette smoke hung in the air.

"Anna called looking for you," she said from behind the counter where she was preparing a fresh pot of coffee. "She told me what happened."

As usual, Rudy's was cold. The condensation covering the plate glass windows made them look like sheets of ice and blurred everything outside into muted masses of shape and color.

"What'd you tell her?"

"Just that I hadn't seen you," she said.

"If she calls again, tell her the same thing," I said.

Carla turned toward me, her brow furrowed, eyes questioning.

My eyebrows shot up. Challenging.

She looked back down at the coffee pot. "Sure," she said softly.

Since I'd moved back to Pottersville, I had spent many nights here in this booth in the back, reading, studying, making case notes and class outlines, and talking to Carla. Most of the time, it was just the two of us, which is why I came. The café sat out on the rural highway, and Rudy, Carla's single father, insisted that it stay open twenty-four hours. And since Rudy was in the back passed out most nights, Carla was the one to keep it open, napping at the bar throughout the night before getting ready and going to school the next morning.

Since like the Pinkertons, I didn't sleep—at least not very much anyway. I came here so Carla could get a few hours in without worrying about getting raped or robbed.

She often thanked me for keeping an eye on the place, either not realizing or not wanting to acknowledge it was her I had come to watch over.

She brought over the coffee pot and two cups.

She wore faded jeans with rips and tears in them, a t-shirt with Amy Lee on it, and inexpensive white tennis shoes that stuck to the sticky floor.

"You can go back to sleep," I said. "I'll be here. Sorry I'm so late tonight."

"But—"

"Actually, you can go in the back and lie down. I can make a pot of coffee if someone comes in. And if something has to be cooked, I'll come get you."

Her sad, sea-green eyes let me know she wanted to stay up and talk, but I didn't want to be around anyone at the moment—not even her.

"You don't want to talk?" she asked.

"Not tonight," I said. "Sorry. Go get some sleep."

As she turned and began to walk away, I called after her. She turned quickly, a hopeful, even expectant look on her face. "Yeah?"

"It's just been a bad day," I said. "Sorry I'm so . . . Thanks for understanding."

"No problem," she said with a small smile. She then continued walking away another step or two before turning around and coming back, taking a seat in the booth across from me. "I know you're . . . but there's something I need to ask you about. I'll be quick."

"Sure, okay," I said.

As far as I knew, I was the only adult she really had to talk to.

She took a deep breath and let it out. "I know we've talked about a lot of stuff, but this is hard."

I waited. I should have encouraged her to continue, reassured her in some way, but I was in no condition to do either.

"I've got a couple of friends whose boyfriends are pressuring them to . . ." she began, then hesitated a moment, before dropping her voice and adding, "have sex with them."

I nodded, trying my best not to convey how very badly I didn't want to do this right now.

"But they want to be virgins when they get married—or at least when they really fall in love and think the guy's the one. So they're considering alternatives—but only because the boys are begging them to. Do you know what I mean by alternatives?"

"Unless your generation has come up with some new ones," I said.

A small smile twitched on her lips. "No, there's just the same old three."

I felt myself getting frustrated, but remembered how much I could have used someone to talk to besides my friends when I was her age.

"Of the three," she said, "they're already doing two. I'm sure you can guess which two. And they think if they do . . . the third one they'll still be virgins and their boyfriends will finally be satisfied."

I shook my head. I couldn't take much more of this. "I know some people claim that anything but vaginal intercourse keeps you a virgin, but those are the same people who put way, way too much emphasis on virginity as some sort of purity test. But that's all sort of moot because the guys pressuring them to do it won't be satisfied. Not for long anyway. Chances are they're gonna always want most what's being kept from them."

She nodded. "That's what I told them. Well, something sorta like that."

"Are we really talking about friends of yours?" I asked.

She nodded slowly. "Yeah. I mean, I've thought about it some too, but I don't even have a very serious boyfriend right now. It really is about two of my friends. I thought if I told them you said it, they'd listen."

I let out a harsh laugh.

"Seriously," she said. "Well, anyway . . . I'll leave you alone now."

As she slid out of the booth, I felt like there was more I should say to her, but I didn't have it in me at the moment.

When she had climbed back onto the bar chair and laid her head down on the counter next to her school books, I said, "Go get in bed. At least get a few good hours."

She glanced toward the back and the small living quarters she refused to call home, then back at me. "I'd rather stay out here."

She was asleep in seconds.

Maybe it wasn't way back when but more recently that I should have been doing more for Carla.

But she's an adult, a mother with a child of her own, and I've tried to walk the fine line between helping her when she would allow and respecting her autonomy.

I kept thinking she's young and would grow up and figure things out, but I should have done more, should have done things differently. The choices she has been making, the way she has been living, the fact that she's missing, all confirm that, don't they?

And just like that, I realize I'm thinking like a controlling, co-dependent, overly-responsible, wannabe savior again.

CHAPTER
TWENTY-NINE

"SHE AIN'T OUT in those swamps," Josh Frye is saying. "I'm tellin' you."

He's a late twenties white man with a military-style buzz cut, small, inset hazel eyes, and over-developed chest and arm muscles.

As if an exaggerated cartoon drawing come to life, his lower body is tiny, especially compared to his chest and arms, and I wonder if he only works out his upper body or if he is unable to bulk up his skinny, bird-like legs for some reason.

He's the correctional officer in charge of the K-9 unit at Gulf CI and the one who ran the dogs at the Hayes's camp searching for Carla.

I am standing in the open bay doorway of the detached garage behind his house beneath the rolled up door. He is leaning over and working on the engine of the '66 Impala he's restoring.

The show car, which is pristine, is a convertible with a deep black finish, a black and gray leather interior, and black chrome wheels.

When I had asked him about it, he had shared with me several details about the 454 big block engine, the ignition, the transmission, the headers, and the suspension that I didn't understand.

"I had a good scent article and Clyde alerted on her scent right away," he is saying, "locked onto it and was gone."

I lean in to hear him better. Somewhere out in the darkness of his backyard from an unseen kennel bloodhounds are barking and baying. Like other K-9 officers in the past, he is raising and training the eventual search dogs from pups.

"No question it was her," he says. "Tracked her like a son of a bitch. He's my best dog. Never gets it wrong."

I nod and encourage him to continue, though his focus is on whatever he's loosening or tightening.

"Hate to see y'all waste time searchin' the swamps when she ain't out there," he says.

I continue to nod and listen.

His garage looks like a showroom, clean, organized, and well appointed.

"I can tell you what she did. She got out of a boat and walked up that path and into the cabin. After that I can't tell you the exact order she did what, but this is what she did. She walked out the back door to the latrine. She walked back into the camp. She walked out the front door and around the side of the cabin, then went into the swamp. I don't know exactly how far she went in or how long she stayed but she went in quite a ways and went around in circles, probably got lost, then she came out about fifty feet to the north of where she went in, then she went back down the path to the river, got in a boat, and left."

Josh seems far more passionate and knowledgable about car restoration than search dogs, and I question many of his conclusions, particularly the certainty with which he states them.

"Clyde tracked her scent back down to the river?" I ask.

"Yeah."

"How can you know it wasn't her scent from arriving and walking up to the cabin?"

"It was in a slightly different spot, and Clyde wouldn't't've gone back down there if she hadn't."

This makes me even more suspicious of everything he's saying, and I wonder if even half of what he's saying is as certain as he's saying it.

"And as far as her scent going back down to the river," I say, "you can't know she got into a boat. She could've gone into the water, right?"

He stands upright, the wrench still in his right hand, frowns, shrugs, and eventually nods slowly. "Yeah, I guess. You think she drowned? That she's in the river?"

I shake my head. "I have no idea where she is. Just tryin' to establish what we can actually know based on what Clyde tracked."

"If she had gone into the water, he would've alerted on it. I've seen him do it before. No, she got in a boat and left."

CHAPTER
THIRTY

"IT HAPPENED AGAIN," Arnie Ward says.

They are the first words out of his mouth when I answer his call.

I know exactly what he's talking about.

"I'm on my way," I say and end the call.

For several months now Arnie has been working on the Olivia Nelson case, and for several months now he's been getting nowhere with it.

Olivia Nelson, a counselor with the school system, is relatively new to town, having moved here about a year ago. And for nearly all that time she has been stalked and harassed by a particularly cunning and prolific predator.

For the first few months the harassment consisted of obscene and threatening phone calls and poison pen letters, but with each successive month the actions of her unknown stalker have escalated, and now include breaking into her home and attacking her.

Arnie had asked if I'd come to the crime scene the next time Olivia was attacked to see if I could help him, and though the timing is terrible I feel obligated to swing by and see if I can offer any assistance before resuming my search for Carla.

I arrive at Olivia Nelson's simple, wooden, ranch style house in Whispering Pines to find Arnie and Darlene standing out front while Olivia receives treatment in the back of an ambulance nearby.

Arnie Ward and Darlene Weatherly are the other two investigators in our agency.

They walk over and meet me as I'm getting out of my truck.

"Thank you for coming, John," he says. "I know you got a lot goin' on, so I won't keep you long."

Arnie Ward, the most senior investigator in our office, is a middle-aged white man, average in every way—average build, clean shaven, clear eyed, a barbershop haircut, drugstore aftershave, sensible shoes, and inexpensive, utilitarian clothes.

He's a good and decent man, conscientious and hardworking. He's the very best I've seen at the paperwork part of the job. His reports and files are thorough and methodical. If a case is straightforward and there's no question as to who the culprit is, he can close it and get a conviction at an extremely high rate, but if it's anything other than that he flounders and often fails.

"I thought we could do a walkthrough of the scene," he says, "and a quick interview of the victim and let you go."

I nod. "Sounds good."

"I asked Darlene to give me her impressions too. Figured between the three of us we can get a handle on this thing before it gets any worse."

I glance at Darlene and nod.

She nods back, but there is obvious tension between us.

Darlene Weatherly is a thick, thirty-something white woman with short hair and a perpetual unpleasant expression. As a deputy, she had helped me on a case I worked in Jackson County several years ago, and I had recommended her for the position she now holds. It was a mistake and I had been wrong to do it. I regret it nearly every day.

She's a lazy, sloppy investigator, an unhappy and jealous

person, and spends far more time attempting to ingratiate herself to the new sheriff than actually doing her job.

"Okay," Arnie says, "let's glove up and go inside."

As we put on shoe coverings and gloves, I glance across the way to Easton and Megan Stevens's house and note its proximity to Olivia's place.

"Any updates on Carla?" Arnie asks as we walk toward the house.

"Not yet."

He nods. "Sorry, John. We're gonna help you with that one too. We'll find her."

Beneath the thick pines, the long, close-to-the-ground ranch looks dated.

He leads us through the open front door, down a short hallway, and into the large, open living room, dining room, kitchen area. One side of the sliding glass door is broken, the shattered glass lying on the tile floor in large jagged shards.

"He breaks in here," Arnie says. "Throws a twenty-pound dumbbell through the glass."

"That he brought with him or was already here?" I ask.

"It was part of a weight set out back," he says. "Belonged to Olivia's ex-husband's dad. This is their house. Well, it was. Roy, Olivia's ex, inherited it and is letting Olivia live in it."

"Where does he live?"

"Tallahassee. That's where she was too until she took the job at the high school and moved here."

"Where is the dumbbell now?" I ask.

He points to the recliner of the seating area over near the couch and the TV. "Rolled under the recliner. She was in the kitchen at the time. Tried to run, but he was already in the living room blocking her way, so she ran back to the kitchen and grabbed a knife. He rushes her. She swings the knife at him. When she misses, he punches her in the face. She goes down, and the next thing she knows he's on top of her holding the knife to her throat."

We step over to the kitchen and look around.

"Crime scene is on the way," he says, "but if it's like before . . . he won't have left any evidence. I'd like to let you hear from her what happened before you go."

I nod, and he leads us back out front and over to the ambulance.

Olivia Nelson has a blanket draped over her shoulders and bandages around her neck and on her left hand. Her left eye has a large purple bruise around it and is swollen shut.

"She needs to go to the hospital," the EMT says. "She has been stabbed in the hand and there was part of a stocking tied so tightly around her neck that it was invisible because the skin covered it."

"I'm not going anywhere," she says. "He's not going to scare me out of my own home."

Olivia Nelson looks like a seventies-era model or actress. She has long, straight black hair and a simple, pure-looking face with no makeup on it, and there's a hint of Native-American ancestry in her features and complexion.

"Who is it?" Darlene asks. "Who did this to you?"

Olivia shakes her head. "I don't know. He wore a mask and gloves and . . . He had on long pants and a long-sleeve shirt. The only part of him that was exposed was a little of his neck."

"What do you remember about that?" Arnie asks.

"He's white, sort of thin, with a protruding Adam's apple."

"Can you tell us what he did and said?" I ask.

"He punched me in the face and jumped on top of me. Took the knife away from me and held the point of it on my throat just beneath my chin. He tied something around my neck and strangled me. It was so tight I thought I was going to die. I did pass out a few times. He whispered everything so I couldn't really get a sense of his voice. He . . . He touched me and smelled me and licked me and kept sayin' I was a dirty slut and asked how it felt to know he was gonna fuck me and kill me."

"Did he rape you?" Darlene says with all the tact and sensitivity of a drunken football fan.

Olivia shakes her head. "No. Never even took my clothes off. He touched me sexually, including with the knife, but it was . . . all of it was through my clothes. Said he was gonna take his time and tonight would just be on-top-of-the-clothes stuff. Like we were teenagers or something."

"Anything about him seem familiar?" I ask. "His size, shape, smell, the way he moved? Anything at all?"

She shakes her head again. "No. Nothing."

Something about the way she said that made me think she knew her attacker or knew more than she was admitting."

"Will you please go to the hospital?" I ask. "Let them take better care of you, and we can protect you better there?"

"I'm not going anywhere. Can someone stay here with me—just tonight?"

"I will," Darlene says. "And I hope to God the bastard comes back. 'Cause I got something for him."

CHAPTER
THIRTY-ONE

LATER THAT NIGHT, with Anna sleeping next to me, I read through Olivia Nelson's case file while trying to fall asleep.

Her harassment began within two months of her moving here.

It began with phone calls—to both her cell and the landline of her ex-in-law's house. Then came the notes and emails.

I wonder how her stalker could have the numbers to her cell phone and her landline—the latter of which was still in her ex-father-in-law's name.

She didn't report it or even tell anyone for the first few months.

She's a proud and private person and found the entire situation embarrassing.

Eventually, inevitably, things began to escalate.

"I would return home from work to find furniture and other household items in different locations from where they were when I left that morning. At first I thought I was just losing it, but eventually . . . I realized someone was breaking into my home while I was gone."

The file contains a transcript of an interview with Olivia and the statement she gave.

"I say break-in, but . . . there was never any sign of . . . forced entry. I started taking pictures with my phone before I'd leave in the mornings, so I'd know exactly where everything was, so I'd have proof that I wasn't going crazy. 'Cause at first I thought I might be."

"That's what he wants you to think," I say.

Beside me Anna stirs. "Huh?"

"Sorry," I say. "I didn't realize I said that out loud."

So, Olivia Nelson's stalker has her cell phone number, the number to the landline of the house she's staying in, and the ability to get in and out of her house without any signs of a break-in.

"It was real subtle—everything he was doing at first. Mostly moving very small items, a pair of earrings or my brush, only short distances. Eventually, it was bigger items moved greater distances. And things started going missing. Mostly articles of my clothing, especially my panties—and not clean ones from my drawer, but dirty ones from my hamper. Well, not dirty. Used. Worn. Pairs I had worn to work and dropped in the hamper when I showered in the evenings. Every few weeks or months he'd do something new, do more, be bolder. Eventually, he started breaking in at night when I was home. I slept with my bedroom door locked, as you can imagine, but when I'd open it in the mornings I'd see he had moved things around. Then he started leaving notes to let me know he had been there."

To this point she had still yet to report any of it or even tell her family and friends.

"Some of the notes were sort of sweet and romantic, but most were threatening and obscene, tellin' me how he was going to fuck me and hurt me and kill me."

Not for the first time Arnie asks her why she didn't report it or at least tell someone. And, as with the times before, she doesn't really give a good answer.

"John."

I turn to see John Paul standing beside our bed.

"Hey buddy. You okay?"

"Had a bad dream."

I sit up and pick him up.

Behind me, Anna turns toward us and says, "What's wrong, buddy?"

"I miss my mommy," he says.

"I know you do, man," I say. "I'm so sorry. I hope she'll be back soon. Do you want to sleep with us tonight?"

He nods his little head.

"Are you ready to go back to sleep yet or do you need to have a snack and talk some first?"

"Snack."

"I'll take him," Anna says.

"No, I got it. Go back to sleep."

"You sure?"

"Yeah. We'll be back in a few. Love you."

"Love you. Thanks. Love you, little buddy. Night."

"Night."

His voice is so small and soft and sleepy it breaks my heart.

CHAPTER
THIRTY-TWO

MY PHONE VIBRATES as I'm driving back to Tupelo Creek the next morning.

I'm meeting Will Hayes at his cabin. Now that crime scene is finished processing the cabin, we'll do a walkthrough to see if anything is missing or out of place.

I glance at my phone. It's Michelle.

"Hey, John. Got a little preliminary info I wanted to share with you. Will get it to you as it comes in instead of waiting to give it all at once."

"I appreciate it."

"How're you holding up?"

"Not great, but it helps to keep moving, keep working everything. Really appreciate all your help and—"

"Of course. Anything I can do, just let me know."

"Thanks."

"I know I've already told you we got no signs of foul play at the cabin, but . . . that's confirmed now and we got no signs of violence or a struggle anywhere—not in the swamp so far, the yard around the cabin, such as it is, the landing, the dock."

"Good."

"We got matches to the footprints from the shoes you

collected from Mason and Lillian, but that still leaves two to three others as yet unidentified. Assuming one of them is Carla . . . we've still got what looks to be one male and one female we haven't identified."

"Can you send me images of the unidentified shoe prints?"

"Sure. Okay, let's see . . . what else? Nothing in Mason's truck or boat. Nothing suspicious. No blood or anything like that. We lifted several prints and collected tons of hairs and fibers, but nothing suspicious. We're running the prints. Will let you know what turns up. Carla was printed when she worked at Head Start, so I'm trying to get those for comparison. Lillian's are on file with the school board. Getting them too. We'll see if any of the others hit anyone in the system. And there were no clothing or personal items or anything that belong to anyone but Mason."

"Okay. That's good to know."

"Vic Roberts says some of the clothing burned in the fire had been new and in good condition. He's trying to see if they can get any other characteristics from it and if there are any biological fluids on it, but he's not very hopeful. He said the accelerant used in the fire was common, garden-variety charcoal lighter. Nothing special about it. Says it's ubiquitous."

An exotic accelerant would've been easier to trace.

"Still no ping on her phone, and none of her credit cards or bank accounts have been used. She hasn't logged in to any of her online accounts."

Before I can respond, another call comes in. I glance at my phone to see it's the sheriff.

"Hey, I've got another call coming in. Thanks for this."

"Sure. I'll let you know when I have something else."

I click over as she ends the call.

"Just got a call from Hank Stevens," Fred Miller says.

Hank Stevens is Easton's dad and a successful local businessman who also happens to be a county commissioner.

"Oh, yeah?"

"Says you're harassing his son and wants it to stop immediately."

"Just the opposite is true," I say. "I had one brief conversation with him and did so in circumstances designed to protect his privacy and maybe save his marriage."

"What's that mean?"

I tell him.

"Okay. Good work. Just tread lightly if or until we have something concrete on him. In the meantime I'll let Hank know the trouble you went to to save his son from embarrassment and tell him politely to fuck off."

As we end the call, I think about the difference in the responses from Mason and Easton's fathers. One is attempting albeit late to make his son be a man and take responsibility for his actions while the other is still intervening to try to ensure there are no consequences. One son might have a chance at becoming a decent human being, but unless something changes the other surely does not.

CHAPTER
THIRTY-THREE

"JUST LET me know if anything is out of place, missing, or if there's something here that's not supposed to be."

Will nods.

As usual, he's wearing loose green scrubs and Crocks. I can't remember a time in the recent past when I've seen him wear anything else. I'm sure he wears them outside of his office to look like a doctor, but they make him look short, slovenly, and emphasize his expanding midsection.

We are on the porch of his cabin.

His face glows redly, as if a combination of sunburn and high blood pressure.

"Okay," he says, nodding, and begins looking around.

His voice is a little raspy, and touching his throat he adds, "Sorry. Too much Karaoke this weekend."

He walks over to a homemade wooden storage box in the far back corner.

Looking down at the empty hasp dangling from a splintered piece of the board, he says, "The lock is missing."

"CSI found a padlock in the swamp to the north."

I pull the evidence bag with the black Master padlock in it out of my pocket and show it to him.

He examines it and nods. "Looks like it."

"Do you have a key so we can be sure?" I ask.

He nods and pulls out his keys. Searching around until he finds the key for the lock, he hands it me. The lock has already been processed, but I still put on gloves to open the bag and try the key. It fits. I return his keys to him.

He looks down at the storage box. "Okay for me to open it?" he asks.

"Everything has been processed," I say. "You can touch anything, do anything you need to."

He leans down and lifts the lid, the metal hinges on the back squeaking as he does, the strong smell of mildew rising out.

"We get broken into all the time," he says. "Most of the camps on the river do. We don't leave much here—and nothing all that valuable. We don't even lock the cabin. We'd rather them not break the windows and doors. This storage box is the only thing we lock."

"Think about what y'all store in here. Anything missing?"

He looks down in the box, then bends down and rummages around in it.

Inside there are a few batteries of difference sizes, some matches and lighters, a couple of bright orange lifejackets, a bottle of sunscreen, a few hats, some canned food, some random clothing, a couple citronella scented candles, and a few cans of insect repellent.

"I can't remember everything that was in here, so there may be more missing than I realize, but . . . there was a pair of jumper cables. I know that for sure. And . . . a few bottles of charcoal lighter. Sure that has nothing to do with Carla bein' missing, but that's all I can tell for sure has been taken."

As he closes the lid, he says, "I feel funny touching things without gloves on. I know it has been processed and . . . and I really hope it's not a crime scene, but still . . . It feels odd."

"I'm still hoping a crime hasn't been committed," I say. "I want her to just show up and be fine."

He nods slowly. "Me too. I . . . I'll . . . I want you to know that I truly don't believe Mason did anything other than leave her here, which is horrible, I know, but . . . He's a spoiled, self-involved boy who hasn't grow up yet, but he's never been violent or even aggressive. He really hasn't."

I nod.

"I'm not just saying that. I know he's my son, but you can ask around. He's never been in a fight."

I nod. "Let's look at the rest of the cabin and see if anything else is missing or out of place."

He heads into the cabin, and I follow.

He stands in the center of the open room and looks around.

"Nothing big is missing or out of place," he says. "There may be a blanket or set of sheets missing. Hard to tell."

He turns and looks at the wall-mounted coat rack near the door. "Might be a raincoat or windbreaker missing. Or one of us may have worn one home and not brought it back. I can ask Beth and Mason if you want me to."

He walks over to the little kitchen area in the back and looks around.

"There may be a few cans of food missing, but it probably just got eaten that last time—Mason probably ate it when he was here."

He turns and looks back at the beds, chairs, and couches that fill the room. "I wonder why he brings girls here. He has such a nice home, but . . . he brings them here."

"His home represents one thing," I say. "This represents something else."

He frowns. "Hope it's not as bad as it seems."

"Could just be an attempt at keeping things casual," I say. "Away from home is away from commitment and domesticity."

He says, "Also means away from his mom's prying eyes."

CHAPTER
THIRTY-FOUR

"I'M surprised to find you here today."

Olivia Nelson looks up from her desk and smiles at me.

Her left eye is blue-black and swollen shut, her right blood-shot and puffy. Her left hand is still bandaged, and she's holding it gingerly.

"Try never to miss work," she says. "Come in. Have a seat."

When she motions to the chair across from her desk with her right hand, she inadvertently moves her left and winces from the pain.

Her small office is in a portable in the back of the high school. The decor she has added makes the space warmer and less commercial, but there is nothing personal in it—no pictures, no passions or interests, only comfort for the kids in crises she spends her days seeing.

"Are young people today suffering from more mental health issues than they were back when we were young or are we just more aware of it?" I ask.

"There's certainly more awareness, but the trauma and anxiety and dysfunction is at a higher level."

"Sure seems like there's so much more than when I was growing up, but I thought I might have just been that obtuse."

"We're seeing the multi-generational impacts of alcoholism and drug-addiction, the breakdown of the family, and, of course, the impacts and amplifications of social media."

I think about Mason Hayes and Easton Stevens.

"I seem to be dealing with so many more cases of narcissism, anti-social tendencies, or at least an extreme form of selfishness —particularly among young men."

She nods. "So much unchecked, toxic masculinity," she says. "Entitled males whose wounded parents don't parent, don't enforce any rules or consequences—and it stretches across all races and socio-economic groups, from frat boys, to rednecks, thugs and gangbangers. It's an epidemic. And now in many cases there aren't functional grandparents to help because of their own issues and addictions. And it's not just the kids I work with. I've gotten involved with many men who have some of these same disorders."

"Do you think one of them could be who attacked you last night?"

She shrugs. "I guess it's possible, but . . . I wouldn't have thought so."

"Do you think the same person is responsible for everything —the stalking, the harassment, the attacks?"

She nods. "Yeah, I guess I do. Haven't really considered it could be more than one person."

"You sure you have no idea who it is?" I ask.

"Have you been assigned to my case?"

"It's still Arnie Ward's case," I say. "I'm just helping out— seein' if a new set of eyes might see something that's been missed."

"Bringing in the big gun," she says. "I'm honored."

"Arnie's our most senior investigator," I say, "I'm just—"

"Everyone knows you're the . . . You're in a league of your own. Solved some high-profile cases."

"All those investigations involved teamwork too. It's how all cases are closed. And that's what we're doing with yours. I hope

I can contribute something so we can end this nightmare for you."

"I'm just hopin' y'all can catch him before he kills me."

"We will," I say. "If you help us."

"What else can I do?"

"We need you tellin' us everything," I say.

"I am."

"Every time we ask you if you know who it is, you change the subject. I asked you if you were sure you didn't know who it was, and instead of answering you asked if I had been assigned to the case. I noticed you did the same type of deflections in your other interviews."

"I don't know who it is."

"You have no idea?"

She hesitates. "If I knew who it was, why wouldn't I tell you?"

"I can think of a few reasons," I say, "but asking me a question instead of answering mine is just more deflection."

"I don't know who it is," she says. "I'm sorry. I wish I did. And I've got students coming in for a support group. Can we talk more later?"

CHAPTER
THIRTY-FIVE

"GOT any thoughts on the Olivia Nelson thing?" Arnie asks.

"Yeah," I say, "but none you haven't had."

"Let me hear them anyway."

"Who would have both the number of the landline and her cell phone number? Who would use both?"

"Her ex-husband."

"Who could get into the house without having to break in?"

"Her ex."

"Why does he let her live in his parents old house?"

"In order to be able to stalk her?"

"Why won't she tell us who it is?"

"That's the part I can't figure out," he says.

"Is her mother still alive?" I ask. "Does she have any siblings."

"Yeah. Until I talked to them, her mother and younger sister knew very little about what's happening to her."

"Either he's threatening them . . ." I say. "Or . . . this is all part of some sick dynamic between her and her ex and some part of her—probably a deeply subconscious part—doesn't want it to end. Or—"

"Hadn't really considered that second one," he says.

"Or . . ." I say again, "she's making it all up."

"All of it?" he asks. "She choking herself and stabbing herself in the hand?"

"It was her left hand," I say. "Nothing's happened to her so far she couldn't do herself. And his escalation doesn't make sense. He breaks in and attacks her—more than once. *Tells* her he's going to rape and kill her but doesn't do either?"

"Definitely doesn't add up, but . . . I never considered she was doing it to herself. I mean . . . claiming you're getting obscene phone calls or someone is following you to get some attention . . . that's one thing, but punching yourself in the eye, choking yourself with a stocking so tight it can't be seen, and stabbing yourself in the hand . . . that's . . ."

"I'm not saying she's doing it," I say. "Just sharing my thoughts so far with you. And even if she *is* doing it all . . . it's entirely possible she doesn't know she is."

CHAPTER
THIRTY-SIX

WHEN I ARRIVE BACK at the landing, I find Anna waiting for me.

I'm so happy to see her the thing Shakespeare said about happiness comes to mind. Altering the line slightly in my mind, it comes out something like this—I were but little happy to see her if I could say how much.

I pull up, park, and leave the truck running. She gets in with me.

"Hey," she says in that sweet, loving, caring way that conveys so much more than a mere greeting. "I had a little free time before picking up the kids and thought I'd check on my baby."

"I'm so glad you did."

We lean in and hug each other, holding on for a long moment.

When we let go, we sit in silence for a while.

The quiet is nice, and her presence is healing.

The landing is roped off, crime scene tape flapping in the breeze, and though there is a lot going on down river around the Hayes' camp and the swamp behind it, there is no activity at the landing just now. Around the perimeter of the cordon, trucks with empty boat trailers and emergency services vehicles sit baking in the ferocious Florida sun.

Beyond the landing, the dark waters of the river bounce and sparkle as the cypress trees lean in as if to watch.

Without me realizing what she's doing, Anna has turned on some soothing music on her phone and placed it on seat between us.

I reach over and take her hand.

Her elegant, narrow fingers are nearly as long as mine and fit perfectly. Our hands hold our history, both individually and as a couple. Since we first began holding hands, their skin has thinned, the veins beneath become more prominent, and additional scars have appeared, and as a result they have become more nurturing, more healing, more comforting, more reassuring.

Eventually she says, "How are you?"

Her voice is soft and tender.

I shrug and frown. "I'm doing my best to not even think about all the dark possibilities, so I'm mostly struggling with what I could've done to prevent her from . . . ever getting into this situation."

"Being on the river with someone who would leave her there?"

"If that's what he did," I say. "Being involved with someone like Mason. And she wasn't just involved with him. She's still been seein' Easton too."

"There's often overlap," she says. "Very few people end one relationship and spend time healing and processing and then when they're ready and have learned all the lessons from the previous one move onto the next."

"True, but—"

"Think about all the issues we had with Chris," she says, referring to her ex-husband.

"Those weren't because you were still sleeping with him— unless there's something you need to tell me. And it's not just that she's sleeping with two guys who are themselves sleeping with other women . . . it's the kind of guys they are."

"The kind who are secretly, selfishly sleeping with multiple women," she says. "The kind who would leave her on the river."

"The kind who are so self-absorbed they treat her like a . . ."

"Sex doll," she says.

"If Mason's tellin' the truth," I say, "and I'm not convinced he is . . . refusing to get in the boat with him, to be discarded after being used, shows she was standing up for herself, demanding better treatment."

"Yes, it does, and that is a direct result of her relationship with you."

I shake my head. "I'm not convinced of that, but even if it is . . . It wasn't enough. I didn't . . . I failed to . . ."

"You've done so much for her," she says. "More than anyone in her life. You have nothing to feel guilty about. You know as well as I do that there's only so much any of us can do. You do more than anyone I know. But you can't fix anyone, can't make them heal or choose a better way. They have to—and it sounds like she was beginning to do that."

"Yeah," I say, "but it's all for nothing if it got her killed."

CHAPTER
THIRTY-SEVEN

"I'VE GOT A LITTLE MORE TIME," Anna says. "You want to talk through things with me?"

We are still sitting in my truck together, holding hands, listening to peaceful, contemplative music, and watching the river.

"Sure," I say. "Thanks."

She knows how much it helps me to say what I'm thinking out loud and to get feedback mostly in the form of questions.

Before I can begin, my phone vibrates.

Glancing at the screen, I see that it's dispatch.

"Let me take this real quick first," I say to Anna, as I answer the call.

"John," Emma Stark, the twenty-something dispatch operator says, "tips are starting to come in. How do you want me to handle them?"

"I'd like to hear them as soon as possible," I say. "Can you email all of them to me and text or call with any that are urgent or seem the most credible?"

"Yeah, I can do that."

"What've we got so far?" I ask.

"Couple of spottings of her vehicle and of her," she says. "You ask me . . . they're not very credible, but . . ."

"Okay," I say. "Just email them to me and we'll follow up on all of them."

"So far the one that seems the most credible is . . . a witness says she saw Carla and another woman havin' a heated argument at the end of the road on Sunday afternoon."

"Who reported it, and did she say who Carla was arguing with?"

"Rhonda Suber called it in, but she didn't say if she knew who it was."

"Okay," I say. "Thanks. Text me that one and email me everything—even the ones you call or text about."

"Will do."

"Thank you, Emma."

When we end the call, Anna says, "I've got fifteen minutes. Lay it out for me."

"If just Carla was missing, it might mean one thing, but with her vehicle missing too . . . it changes the possibilities and how we have to approach the investigation. Could she have come out of the swamp and off of the river, gotten into her vehicle, and driven away or . . . Did someone take her and her vehicle? Or do something to her and hid her vehicle? Either way . . . where is her vehicle? We have every law enforcement agency looking for it. If it were on the road, I think we would've found it by now."

She nods and seems to be thinking about it but doesn't say anything.

"The footprints at the cabin tell us Carla and Mason weren't the only ones who were there, but we can't know when the other prints were made. Could be before they were there and have nothing to do with her disappearance or could be after Mason was gone—if he really left without her—and could belong to whoever has her."

"What were Mason's VSA results?"

"Indicate he lied about a lot but seem to suggest he wasn't being deceptive about leaving her there."

"Doesn't mean he couldn't've gone back."

"True."

"What else?"

"If Josh Frye is right—"

"Who?"

"The new K-9 officer at Gulf. If he's right that she went into the swamp . . . Why? Did she go with someone? By herself? Was she chased? Did she really come out or is she still in there? He says she came out, but . . . I'm not sure how much of what he says to believe. He definitely says things with certainty he can't know. The path he said she took has no signs of violence on it. Neither does the cabin or Mason's truck and boat."

"Maybe she came out and is missing for other reasons," she says.

"It's possible. It's what I keep holding onto, but . . . It seems unlikely. Especially with the fire at the McDaniels's cabin. If someone burned her clothes or his or both, it was to hide evidence."

"Or maybe the fire has nothing to do with her," she says.

"Maybe."

We are quiet a moment.

"I feel like I'm too . . . Like I'm not thinking straight, not processing information or clues like I usually do."

"Because it's Carla?"

I nod. "I've been trying to compartmentalize and not even think about it being her, but I must not be. I'm just not getting anywhere."

"It's still early, and you have very little to go on," she says. "You'll get it. You will. I'm gonna go take good care of our children. You do what you need to find her. Don't think about or worry about anything else. Just focus on finding her. You're the best hope she has."

CHAPTER
THIRTY-EIGHT

AS I HEAD BACK toward my truck from walking Anna to her car and kissing her goodbye, I look around at the vehicles parked around the landing and wonder again at what happened to Carla's car.

If it was out on the road, it would have been spotted by now —unless it's way away from here. Had it been driven out of the area before we ever started looking for it? And if so, by Carla or someone else?

Or maybe it's hidden in someone's garage. Did someone abduct Carla and take her vehicle too? Could she be in some sadist's dungeon right now, her car beneath a tarp in his yard?

If someone took her and her car, he'd either have to have help or have to come back for a vehicle—either hers or his. If he lived close enough, he could walk back to collect the second vehicle. Our canvas of the area hadn't turned up anything suspicious so far. None of the deputies or investigators conducting the house to house have raised any concerns about anyone's behavior or flagged anyone who warrants a followup.

But what if an abductor didn't have help and didn't live close by? Or what if Mason or someone else did something to Carla at the camp or on the river or in the swamp and had to get rid of her car? What would they do? How would they do it without help?

I hope Carla is somewhere in her car, but with each passing moment the chances of that become less and less likely.

What would someone do to quickly and effectively get rid of Carla's car?

Driving it down the boat ramp and into the water is the most obvious, but the landing isn't deep enough. The car would be visible. And even if some part of it might actually be deep enough to cover the top of her car, the boats launching would run into it. This landing is just too small and shallow to—

I stop walking and look over at the narrow dirt road on the south side of the landing.

It runs parallel to the river and leads to the lower landing— an unofficial dirt landing not maintained by the county, one that is large enough and deep enough to hide a vehicle in.

The road and the lower landing have been searched, but the water hasn't. And unless Carla's car is somewhere far away or hidden in a garage I'd put money on it being in there.

Of course, there's another possibility.

Instead of her would-be attacker or abductor driving her car into the river at the lower landing, she could've done it.

If her car is there, it may not just be her car.

She might have been chased and drove it in. She could've been disoriented and thought she was driving away from Tupelo Creek.

I look around at the landing again, see the members of the media set up on the north side of the yellow crime scene tape.

I want to do a search of the lower landing without them knowing anything about it.

Pulling out my phone, I call Kent Roberts, the member of Search and Rescue who is the best with sonar scanning.

"Can you meet me at the lower landing?" I ask.

"Yeah, sure. Give me a—"

"Don't mention it to anyone, and come in from the river so the media won't see you."

"You got it."

CHAPTER
THIRTY-NINE

UNLIKE THE UPPER LANDING, the lower one is more isolated, overgrown, untouched, natural. Essentially it's a dirt road that doesn't end until it reaches the water.

I'm waiting at the water's edge for Kent when he pulls up.

"Has this landing been scanned?" I ask.

He shakes his head. "Not yet."

"Can we do it now?"

"Sure. Get in."

Kent's small boat is equipped with sonars mounted on the sides and monitors mounted in the middle. And it's lighter and smaller than I thought it would be, resembling an oversized, inflatable kayak.

Sonar is a technology that sends a signal underwater then displays a reading by receiving its echo. The echo of the ping is created when the original signal bounces off the bottom and objects in the water column between the transducer and the bottom. It's used to detect water depth and the presence of objects in the water.

"We want to go upstream," he says. "Against the current so we have more control over the boat. We want to scan at a speed of between 1.9 to 2.5 miles per hour."

He finishes preparing his equipment and drops the sonars into the water.

"We've got side and down sonar running," he says, nodding toward the screen.

One of the mounted monitors displays a split screen—one showing a graphic of the boat on a black background with large gold boxes extending out on each side, the other showing black above what looks like a field of glowing gold corn stalks. The other, which isn't as clear and resembles more a doctor's office sonogram, is from the live scope.

"Everything black is water," he explains. "The gold is riverbed. This image extending out from the boat on this one is the side scan sonar. It reaches about seventy-five feet on each side. This other is the down sonar. That's directly beneath the boat. The other monitor is a live view. It's a little harder to read but more immediate."

I nod. "Thanks."

"Won't take us long to scan this area," he says. "Not much to it."

I want to find Carla and her vehicle more than anything right now, but not here, not submerged beneath the black waters of the Miccosukee River.

"When a vehicle goes into the water, it's going to be moved some by the current—depending how fast it was going, how far it went in, and the speed of the current, but once it settles on the bottom it's going to stay where it is. It won't move after that. We'll start about where I think a vehicle would come to rest if it was driven into the water here."

He maneuvers the boat over to a spot about twenty-five feet from the boat ramp and begins his scan.

"I'll be surprised if there's not several things down here," he says. "Old boat or two, fallen trees, maybe even an old vehicle."

He studies the monitors as we slowly ease up stream.

He is very practiced and methodical, guiding the boat in strait rows as if tilling the ground for a garden.

"See that?" he says, pointing toward a spot on the monitor.

I follow his finger to a raised area in the gold section.

"That's probably an old boat. We're seeing the side of it. You can tell by the angle and size—and it has been down there a while. Got a lot of sediment on it."

I am unable to tell any of that from the image he's pointing at, but I know he knows what he's talking about.

"Over there—see that," he says, pointing to another spot on the side scan sonar. "That looks like a very old truck. We'll know more when we get over there on top of it. But—"

He stops and turns his attention to the live scope monitor.

"That's . . . Look at that."

He kills the motor and drops an anchor.

"That's a . . . we're directly on top of a newer car. It's . . . How deep is it here? Fourteen-four."

My heart seems to sink into the empty abyss that is now below it.

"See?" he says, reaching over and pointing to a spot on the other monitor.

I see what he's pointing to, and it does look different from the area around it, but nothing about it resembles a car to me.

"It's upside down," he says. "See the tires sticking up—here and here."

I see something that slightly resembles a gold and black tire coming in and out of the undulating signal.

"We found it," he says. "That's . . . I'd be willing to bet that's Carla's car."

He reaches past his dive equipment, grabs a magnet the size of a couple of hockey pucks on a line, and drops it into the water.

"We need to get the dive team down here," he says.

"I want to go down first," I say. "See for myself."

"What? No. I promise you you don't."

"I do. I've got to."

"Do you even know how to dive?"

"Yeah. It's been a while, but yeah."

"Diving in the river is dangerous, plus visibility is zero. And if she's been in there a couple of days you don't want to see her."

"You're right. I don't want to. But I have to."

CHAPTER
FORTY

I STOPPED DIVING several years ago primarily because of sinus issues and the havoc the water pressure wreaked on my head.

I had returned to the surface too many times with blood in my mask and skull-splitting headaches.

I'm out of practice and was never very skilled to begin with, but I remember enough to go see for myself if Carla and her car are submerged here, buried in this watery grave.

I adjust my BC, make sure the tank is secure, and ease into the water holding my mask.

The wetsuit is very tight, and the mask and fins and weight belt don't fit quite right, but I don't want to take any additional time to adjust anything—and I'm not sure how much difference additional adjustments would make.

In the water, I wash off the mask and put it on, then do the same with the regulator.

"I only have this for emergencies," Kent says. "Probably not much left in that tank."

I check the gauge. He's right. It's in the red. Depending on my breathing, I only have a few minutes.

He leans over and hands me down the underwater dive light with the pistol grip.

"Need to get down there and back up here as quickly as possible," he says.

I give him the okay sign.

Releasing the air out of the BC, I begin to sink.

My descent is faster than I would like, and I can feel the pressure in my head immediately.

I'd like to slow it down but don't feel as though I can.

I realize I'm breathing rapidly and attempt to slow my heart rate and breathing.

Visibility is even worse than I had imagined. There is nothing but blackness everywhere—except directly in front of the beam of my dive light.

It doesn't take long to cover the fourteen feet or so between the surface and the riverbed.

When I reach the bottom, I realize I've drifted away from the vehicle—or was never directly over it to begin with.

I shine the light around and turn slowly in every direction.

Nothing.

I begin to swim around, searching, feeling with one hand, shining the light with the other.

I become aware of breathing too rapidly again and attempt to relax and breathe more slowly.

My nose is bleeding—something I feel rather than see.

I can't believe I can't find the vehicle. It should be right here.

I may have drifted even farther than I realized, and now that I've been swimming around in the dark I have no idea where I am in relation to the boat above, no bearings, no points of reference, no clue. And I'm running out of air.

I change directions again and continue to feel my way around, floating about three feet from the bottom.

The beam of the bright light finds trash and debris and downed trees but no vehicles.

Wondering how much air I have left, I grab my gauge and bring it around to check it.

And as I'm trying to see it, I bump into the rear quarter panel of the passenger's side of Carla's gray Camry.

Dropping the gauge, I bring the light around and begin to search the car, my vision blurring from the tears in my eyes.

The vehicle is upside down on a slight incline, its back tires about a foot higher than the front.

The bright light finds John Paul's initials on the back window and the dent in the back bumper, but it didn't need to for me to know it's Carla's car.

Running out of air, I quickly search the vehicle, starting in the back.

The trunk is open.

I shine the light inside it.

It's empty except for a small plastic crate and some random clothes and shoes, a few of which are on the riverbed below it.

Making my way around to the driver's side, I see that the front window on that side is open—not broken, but rolled down.

Taking a breath and preparing myself for what I might find, I swim down to the window and look inside.

The first thing I see is one of John Paul's toys, a bright yellow dinosaur floating above the steering wheel.

Other items float around the interior of the upside down vehicle—empty soda bottles, a sneaker, a Styrofoam food container, more toys, more trash, a pair of jeans shorts.

In the backseat the straps from John Paul's carseat hang down toward the roof.

The front passenger side door window is halfway down, but the two back windows are up.

Carla is not inside the vehicle.

Was she ever?

Had she been in it when it went into the water? Had she been alive and escaped through the open window? Had she been dead and eventually floated out?

Or had someone driven her vehicle in here to hide it and swum out once it was in the water?

I want to search the area for her body. I want to search the car for signs of violence or clues as to what happened, but I'm out of air, and now both my nose and ears are bleeding and I must re-inflate my BC and swim for the surface.

CHAPTER
FORTY-ONE

"GOOD WORK," Fred Miller says softly as he walks up.

Michelle and I are standing at the lower landing, watching as the winch on the large black and white tow truck slowly pulls Carla's car from the water.

It's early evening, and the sinking sun burnishes the delicate surfaces of flowers and leaves with a warm orange tint and suffuses the atmosphere with a soft golden glow.

A Search and Rescue boat is in the river not far from the car, a diver is in the water, and various deputies, emergency service personnel, and FDLE crime scene techs, and members of Search and Rescue are standing on the sides of the boat launch, all watching as the river is forced to give up the vehicle.

The landing is quiet, the only consistent sound in the hush of the gloaming being the monotonous whine of the electric winch motor and the metallic twitching tension on the cable extending from it to Carla's car.

Everyone looking on does so reverently as if they believe a body to be inside the vehicle.

"No sign of the . . . of Carla?" Miller asks.

I shake my head.

"What're we thinkin'?" he asks.

"Driver's window is down," I say. "Whoever was in it—Carla or someone else—could've been conscious and swum out as the car sank. Or . . . if whoever was in it was . . . unconscious, their body could've floated out later."

"We need Search and Rescue to drag the river in case that's what happened," he says.

I nod. They already are.

He says, "Finding her vehicle here will give them new parameters to focus their search."

He frowns and nods slowly and says, "I hope . . . she's not . . . that she's not . . . in the river."

Michelle says, "FDLE is going to take possession of the vehicle and process it. We should know more about who was in it once they have."

"Good," he says, nodding more quickly. "That's good."

We are quiet for a moment.

"I guess . . ." Miller says, "the thing to hope for is that she was in the vehicle and got out or never in it to begin with. If someone else was . . . it means they wanted to hide it for some reason. And if she was . . . unconscious or . . . Anyway . . . Praying for her safety. John, can I see you for a minute before I head back to the office?"

I walk over to his SUV with him.

"I understand you dove down to the vehicle when you found it," he says.

"I did."

"I wish you hadn't done that," he says. "I understand . . . you wanting to, but . . ."

I nod.

"There's a reason why we don't work the cases that involve people we're close to."

"I won't do anything like that again," I say.

"I feel like you'd . . . that it'd be better for you to work something else right now."

I can't not work Carla's case. I've got to convince him to leave me on it.

"Please," I say. "Let me stay on this. I won't do anything like that again. I can stay objective. I can . . . please let me keep working this. I'll treat it like any other case. I will."

He looks as if he's contemplating his decision.

"Please," I say.

What will I do if he takes me off of it? Work it anyway? Quit and work it independently? And if I do, how will Anna and I pay for Nash to go to college or anything else?

Eventually, he nods slowly. "Okay. For now. But make sure you . . . I don't want to have to pull you, but I won't have any choice if you . . ."

"I won't," I say.

When he is gone, I walk over to Carla's car, snapping on gloves as I do.

The Camry is on land now, moving slowly toward the tow truck at the top of the boat launch, river water leaking out.

I motion for the tow truck operator to stop.

He does.

Michelle walks over to me. "FDLE is going to process the car."

"I know," I say. "I just want a quick look inside before they take it."

"Be careful," she says.

I walk around the exterior of the vehicle to check for damage.

Seeing John Paul's initials on the back window makes my heart ache for him, and I resolve to get home early enough to spend time with him and the rest of my family before they go to bed.

There's no obvious new or unexplainable damage to the vehicle.

I walk back around to the driver's window and look inside.

Leaning down into the open window, I am assaulted by the odor of mildew and the strong stench of soured and rotting waterlogged cloth and fabric.

I scan the entire vehicle.

There's still a foot or more of standing water in the floor-boards, but unless something's hidden in there I don't see anything in the car I wouldn't expect to be there.

Glancing down at the driver's seat, I can tell it has been adjusted.

Opening the door just enough for the water to flow out more quickly but not far enough for any objects inside to spill out, I wait for the water to drain. Once it has, I open the door the rest of the way.

Squatting down to more closely examine the seat, I can see that it's positioned back as far as it can go.

"What is it?" Michelle asks.

"Carla is on the short side," I say. "Has to have her seat moved forward to reach the pedals. The seat is set as far back as it can go."

"So she didn't drive it into the river," she says.

"Exactly. Doesn't necessarily mean she wasn't inside the vehicle at the time, but it does mean she wasn't driving."

CHAPTER
FORTY-TWO

"JOHN, can I be Chunky for Halloween?" John Paul asks.

We are lying in his bed, and I'm reading *Pumpkin Jack* by Will Hubbell to him.

It's his favorite book, one we read year round, and even though Halloween is over two months away, it has him thinking about his costume.

Anna is helping Taylor get ready for bed. Johanna and Nash are in their rooms.

"Sure," I say. "Who is that?"

"Chunky," he says again, as if it's obvious.

"Is he or she from a cartoon or a book or a video or a game?"

He gives his little shoulders a shrug.

"What does he look like? Where did you see him?"

"You know . . ." he says. "Chunky."

"Can you describe him to me?"

I pull out my phone and search Chunky kids character.

Nothing that remotely resembles a kids' character comes up in the search results.

I click over to Youtube, and say, "Is he from a video you watch?"

"Yeah," he says. "On mommy's phone."

I type Chunky into the Youtube search bar.

A Bruno Mars song comes up, followed by Trampsta, an old black and white film dance, then a clip from Madagascar.

"Is this it?" I ask, pointing at the Madagascar image.

He shakes his head. "We need mommy's phone."

"Yes, we do," I say.

"I miss her. When is she coming back?"

"I'm not sure, but I hope very soon. I'm sorry she's not here right now, but let's see if we can get my phone to work like hers, okay?"

He nods his little head and says "Okay" in such a soft, sweet little voice that my eyes begin to sting.

"Chunky," he says again. "And the bride."

"Do you mean Chucky?" I say.

"*Yeah.*"

"The little doll?"

"*Yeah.*"

Carla lets him watch content I wouldn't, but I can't imagine she'd let him watch that.

"Have you watched Chucky or just seen a picture?"

"My mommy was watching it on her phone. She stopped it, but I saw him."

He likes dark, suspenseful, and scary stories, and I'm not surprised he'd be drawn to the image of a doll that embodies all those things.

I bring up an image of a Chucky doll on my phone.

"This?" I ask.

"Yeah. Can I be that for Halloween this year?"

"We'll talk to your mommy about it," I say. "You still have plenty of time to decide. Halloween is two months away."

"Okay."

"What're y'all reading?" Taylor asks, as she walks in. "Let me guess. Jack Pumpkin."

She is freshly bathed and in her unicorn nightgown.

"I'm gonna be Chunky for Halloween," John Paul says.

"You should be Jack Pumpkin as much as you like that."

I don't remind her it's *Pumpkin Jack*.

Anna walks in a moment later. She looks tired and ready for bed herself. Not only does she have an extra child to care for, but I haven't been helping as much as I normally do over the past couple of days.

"One more book then lights out," she says. "What do y'all want to read?"

"Percy Jackson," Taylor says.

"Pumpkin Jack," John Paul says.

"We can do *Pumpkin Jack* since your . . ." Taylor says. "*Pumpkin Jack* is fine."

"Thank you, sweet girl," I say. "That's very kind of you. Do you know what you want to be for Halloween this year?"

"Either a dead Disney princess or a zombie rock star."

"Cool," I say. "Can't wait to see that."

She and Anna climb into the bed with us, and we snuggle up and I read *Pumpkin Jack* for the thousandth time, but this time the words are a little blurry.

CHAPTER
FORTY-THREE

WITH MY FAMILY FAST ASLEEP, I go back to work.

Getting in my truck, I drive the short distance to the liquor store on Main.

It's late. The streets are empty. It had rained earlier, and the air is thick with moisture and a faint, lazy fog.

The wet surfaces of the small town refract street lamps, headlights, and the only traffic light, which at this time of night becomes a caution light flashing yellow and red.

Standing water in the storm drain runoffs and the random puddles provide a shimmering, fractured mirror image of the convenience store sign and the gas prices it's advertising.

The water residue on my windshield and the light fog make everything look smudged and impressionistic.

Where is Carla on this wet night? Is she still alive? Is she frightened? In pain?

Good Spirits is a small, cinderblock-building liquor store on Main Street next to the substation with a drive-thru beneath a covering that resembles a carport.

I pull beneath the covering and up to the window.

Rhona Suber slides the window open and smiles at me.

She's a middle-aged woman carrying at least fifty pounds of extra weight in the bottom half of her body. Beneath her big black mass of teased hair, a thick layer of make-up covers her full face. And as usual she's adorned with cheap, tinkly jewelry— several earrings in her ears, clusters of bracelets around her wrists, necklaces of varying lengths, and at least one ring on every finger.

She starts to ask what she can get me but stops and gives me a pitiable expression.

It's obvious she thinks I'm here for alcohol.

I used to battle alcohol addiction or at least alcohol abuse, but that seems like a lifetime ago now. I haven't abused alcohol in many, many years, and I can't imagine ever doing so again.

She shakes her head. "I'm not gonna—We're closed."

"I'm not here for a drink," I say.

"Thank God. Honey, I thought you had fallen off the wagon."

"You reported seeing someone arguing with Carla Pearson," I say.

"Oh, yeah. At the end of the road. I was just driving by— turning off of Byrd Parker onto the dam road. Didn't see much. They were a good ways away, but they were in each other's faces. Look like they were about to fight."

"When was this?"

"Sunday . . . around . . . It was in the early afternoon. I can probably narrow it down if you need me to. I had to be into work at one, and I ran by the Dollar Store for snacks on my way in, so . . . probably around 12:30 or so."

A car with a belt slipping pulls in behind me.

"I'll circle around and let you wait on them," I say.

She nods.

I pull out of the liquor store parking lot onto Second Street, take a left, then another left on Court, another on Main, and then another back into the Good Spirits parking lot behind the car that is now at the window.

When the car pulls out, I pull back up to the window.

"You know . . ." she says, "I said they were arguing, but that's not really it. Carla was sort of leaning back. It was like the other woman was attacking or threatening her. I don't think she was . . . I don't think they were arguing . . . I think the other woman had beef with Carla. Not the other way around."

"Who was the other woman?"

She shakes her head and shrugs. "Her back was to me. I only saw them for a moment."

"But you're sure it was Carla?"

"Got a good look at her. She was facing me. But the other woman . . . Her back was to me."

"Can you describe her to me?"

She frowns and shrugs.

"How tall was she in comparison to Carla? Was she thin or heavy or—"

"She was taller than Carla—"

"Then how'd you see Carla's face?"

"She was at an angle to me. I'm positive it was Carla. I saw her good. The other woman was a little taller than Carla and a little heavier but not much—of either."

"Any idea who it could've been?"

She frowns and shakes her head.

"If you had to guess—who comes to mind?"

"I can't come up with a name, but she seemed like one of these young mothers or professional women around town. The younger generation. Like maybe she worked at the bank or co-op or was a teacher or something."

Easton's wife, Meg, is a teller at the credit union and Mason's not so ex-girlfriend, Lily, is a teacher.

Was it one of them? Did they have a confrontation with Carla at the landing and then later follow her and Mason to the camp?

"Okay. Thanks. That's very helpful."

"Probably had nothing to do with her goin' missing, but . . . thought I should let y'all know."

"Very glad you did. Call me if you think of anything else.

And I'll probably bring some photos by at some point and see if any of them might be her."

CHAPTER
FORTY-FOUR

MY PHONE VIBRATES as I'm pulling out of the Good Spirits parking lot.

It's dispatch. I answer it.

"Just received a 911 call from Olivia Nelson reporting someone trying to break into her house," Emma Stark says. "A deputy and Arnie are en route. Arnie said to let you know."

"Thanks. Let him know I'm on my way."

I turn on my emergency lights and race through our empty little town toward Whispering Pines.

Arriving first, I park out front and run toward the house.

Seeing no sign of a break-in, I call Olivia.

"Are you okay?"

"Yeah."

"I'm in your yard."

"He's in the back, just beyond the tree line."

"Okay. Stay inside."

The backyard is about an acre of scattered pines, a storage shed, weight pile, and a kids' rotting treehouse.

The lot behind it has yet to be cleared and is wooded and thick with undergrowth.

Running toward it, I see that there are not one but two flash-light beams moving about, and I wonder if Arnie or the deputy parked on the other side of the wooded lot and are approaching from that direction.

I call Arnie as I near the wooded lot.

"We're pulling up now," he says.

"Where?"

"Out front."

"Where is the deputy?"

"Right behind me."

"There are at least two of them and they're in the wooded lot behind Olivia's. I'm approaching them now. Can y'all come around to the other side and enter from there?"

"You got it."

"Leave the deputy's cruiser out front with the lights flashing and let him ride with you."

"Good idea. We're on the way."

"And don't shoot me."

"Don't shoot us."

When I look at the uncleared lot again, I see that one of the lights is headed in the direction of the other.

I head in the same direction, hoping to converge on the two lights as they come together.

Approaching the two lights with my light off, I move slowly through the thick woods, feeling my way from pine to pine, my hands getting sticky with sap.

As I get closer, I lose track of the lights.

Moving blindly now, I continue in what I believe to be the same direction I was headed before—but I can't be sure.

I hear movement up ahead, footfalls, snapping twigs, and a rustling in the thick understory.

I pull out my gun and light and am about to turn on my light and identify myself when I'm struck on the back of the head and go down hard.

The jolt ripples through my entire body. I feel dazed and impaired, but I don't pass out, and though I drop my light I manage to maintain my grip on my gun.

"Gulf County Sheriff's Investigator," I say. "Freeze."

I hear footfalls running in one direction and a rustling in the bushes in the other.

I feel around for my light.

When I find it, I click it on and look up to see a tall, thin, older man stepping toward me.

He's holding a flashlight, but it's not on.

"Are you okay?" he asks.

"Freeze," Javar Williams says as he comes up behind him, light up, weapon drawn. "Hands up."

Javar is a deputy in uniform, a late-twenties African-American man of average height and build.

"John, you okay?" Arnie says coming up behind him. "Here, let me help you up."

As he helps me to my feet and the pine trees swirl around me, Javar tells the older man to put his hands behind his back.

"I will not," he says. "You're not going to cuff me like some common criminal. I haven't done anything wrong."

"Trespassing and battery on a law enforcement officer for starters," Javar says.

"I'm not trespassing," he says. "This is my land. And I didn't touch him. I found him this way."

Arnie whips around toward him. "Roy?"

I assume he means Roy Nelson, Olivia's ex.

"What're you doing here?"

"Looking out for Olivia," he says. "Trying to catch whoever's harassing her."

"Who's with you?" I ask, steadying myself against a thick-bodied pine.

"No one. It's just me."

Arnie looks at me.

"Someone else was here," I say. "There were two lights."

"That was probably Olivia's stalker. Bet that's who hit you on the head. And y'all let him get away."

CHAPTER
FORTY-FIVE

"DID Y'ALL GET HIM?" Meg Stevens asks.

I'm standing on her porch, and she's in her open doorway in pajamas.

She has shoulder-length blond hair, big, blue eyes, and perfect, bright-white teeth seen often in the flash of her quick and easy smile.

Her pajamas are simple—soft gray shorts and a matching t-shirt with teal moon and stars on it. They're not meant to be sexy, but they fit her runner's body as if tailored for it.

"Who?" I ask.

"Poor Olivia's stalker," she says. "We've been tryin' to keep an eye out. Easton went out there with his rifle when we saw the light but came back in when y'all showed up."

"Did y'all see anything?" I ask.

"Just the light moving through that lot. I wish they'd clear it. 'Specially now."

"Have you seen anyone over there or anything suspicious?"

She shakes her head. "No, but I'm not here a lot. Either at the credit union or running or church. When I *am* here I don't usually look out the windows—until lately."

I pull out my phone and pretend to be reading a text, but actually open my camera app.

"Could I speak to your husband for a minute?" I ask.

"Of course," she says.

As she turns to go get him, I snap pictures of her from behind to use in a photo array to see if Rhonda Suber can identify who was threatening Carla on Sunday.

"Easton," she yells. "Door."

"Huh?"

"Door. Police."

She looks back at me. "He'll be down in a minute. Well, goodnight. I'm going back to bed unless you need me for anything else."

"Night," I say. "Thanks for your help. And for keeping an eye on Olivia's place."

"No problem. Wish we could do more."

She climbs the stairs, and in another minute or so Easton comes down them.

When he reaches me, he steps out onto the porch and closes the door behind him.

"What were you doing in the wooded lot behind Olivia's house with a light and a gun?" I ask.

"Looking for—we saw someone over there with a light. Thought it was her stalker."

"Why didn't you call the police?"

"We did. Meg did while I went over there. They told her y'all were already aware of it and on the way."

"Who saw the light?"

"I did."

"Did Meg see it?"

He shrugs. "I told her to call the police and went over there. Don't know what she saw after that."

"Did you see the other person in the woods?"

"No. I followed his light, but then heard y'all and saw the

blue light flashing in Olivia's front yard, so I let y'all have it. Didn't want to get shot."

"Or hit on the back of the head," I say.

"Or anything."

"Why'd you hit me?" I ask.

"Huh?" he says. "I didn't. What're you—"

"So we won't find my blood on the stock of your rifle," I say.

"I . . . I didn't know it was you. I swear. I thought it was the . . . stalker. That's why I took off. Sorry about that. It was just an accident. Please don't make a thing of it."

"You ever see anyone over at Olivia's or in that lot before?"

"Her ex works on the place sometimes. Nobody else really."

"A woman was seen threatening Carla at the end of the road on Sunday afternoon," I say. "The description fits Meg."

"What? No. No way. She wasn't even there. She was at church."

"This was after church. Probably shortly after you dropped Carla back there."

"It wasn't her. She doesn't know. She wouldn't . . . No way it was her."

"You sure she doesn't know?"

"Positive. She would've kicked me out."

"Maybe she decided to handle it a different way."

He shakes his head. "Absolutely not. No fuckin' way. Not in her nature."

"I've kept your little secret," I say. "But if you lie to me again or if you have your daddy call the sheriff for you I'm gonna have a serious talk with your wife. Understand?"

CHAPTER
FORTY-SIX

"I'M WORRIED ABOUT HER," Roy Nelson is saying. "I still care about her, and she's in real trouble."

A good bit older than Olivia, he's a tall, trim man in his sixties with thickish gray hair that's longer than it is stylish. It's probably just the bad lighting, but his eyes look gray also.

Arnie, Javar, and I are standing around him near Arnie's car on the edge of the wooded lot that is opposite of Olivia's house.

"You're stalking her because you're worried about her?" I ask.

"I'm not stalking her," he says. "I'm not stalking anyone. Unless you count . . . I'm stalking her stalker."

Everything about the way he speaks—the diction, pronunciation, accent, and cadence—lend a certain weight to his words. He's a distinguished psychologist and professor, a man who spends a lot of time talking, one who expects to be listened to.

"Oh," I say, "you're stalking her stalker."

Javar shakes his head. "That's not a thing," he says. "Stalking a stalker."

"I'm just trying to protect her. All I meant was I was watching the place in case the guy tried to break in again. That's it. I should've let y'all know. I didn't think anyone would even see me. All I was doing was watching. It's my house. It's my property. I own the wooded lot too. I can do anything I want to there."

"Then why not clear it so creeps can't use it for cover?" I ask.

"It's already in the works."

"Do you have a key to the house?" I ask.

"Of course."

"Do you ever go in when Olivia's not there?"

"On occasion," he says. "To let repair people in or to get something out of storage. She doesn't mind. Hell, she asks me to take care of things from time to time. But I always let her know when and what I'm doing."

Arnie says, "Are you spying on your ex? You jealous? Want to see who she's seeing? That why you have her in your house?"

"I don't *have her* in my house," he says. "I'm letting her use my parents' old place. I'm not jealous or spying or stalking. I care for Olivia. I do. And I feel bad for her. She's quite vulnerable, but . . . be clear on this. I broke up with her. She'd get back together with me tonight if I wanted it. I don't. I'm seeing someone else. And, to be honest, I was seeing her before I broke things off with Olivia. I'm not trying to get her back or control her or anything else. I'm just worried about her."

Something occurs to me, and I decide to ask him even though I should look into it first.

"Was or is Olivia one of your patients?" I ask.

"I . . . I can't reveal anything about my patients—even if it's to say who isn't one."

"Have you prescribed medications for her?"

"I can't reveal anything about my practice or my patients," he says. "You know that."

"Who do you think's harassing her?" I ask.

He shakes his head. "No idea. I wish I did. All I know is it's not me. And you know how you can know that? Ask her. She knows me very well. We were together for several years. She'd know if it were me. Even with a mask on."

Arnie says, "How do you know her attacker wore a mask?"

"She told me. I mean really, is this all you have? She's in real danger and y'all are harassing the one person trying to help her."

CHAPTER
FORTY-SEVEN

"WE'RE GOING to have to end the ground search here today," Fred Miller is saying.

"Should have two days ago," Josh Frye, the K-9 officer from the prison says. "I keep tellin' y'all she left here."

We are standing on the dock in front of the Hayes's river camp, the boats tied to it bobbing in the water as it slaps their hulls.

Tom Dickinson, the head of Search and Rescue, says, "We'll keep dragging the river—for at least the rest of this week."

"Obviously," Miller says, "we haven't searched every square inch of the swamp behind the cabin, but we've done a pretty damn thorough search, and she's just not here. Dogs say she's not. Our searches haven't turned up a single sign that she's out there—or ever was." He looks at me. "I know you'd like for us to keep searching, but . . . I just feel our resources would be better spent . . . elsewhere."

"Where?" I ask.

"Meeting in my office first thing in the morning to discuss that," he says.

Michelle Quinn says, "It's important to remember this doesn't mean our search for Carla stops. It just stops in this location. And with all the evidence pointing to her not being here, searching other places and intensifying the investigation puts us in a better position to find her."

I nod. I don't disagree with what they're saying, but they're arguing their points as if they have to talk me into it.

"Okay," Miller says. "Let's get back to work. Make today count. End strong here. And be thinking of where the investigation and search needs to go next. Bring your ideas to the meeting in my office in the morning."

Everyone disperses—some to the back of the house and the search still taking place there, others leaving by boat, returning to the landing.

Eventually, I am alone on the dock.

Taking several deep breaths, I attempt to clear my head and empty my mind.

I look out at the wide river. The midmorning sun emphasizes the greenish hue in the otherwise light-gray and brown waters.

Beyond the smooth surface of the water meandering toward the bay, the dense river swamp on the opposite bank is untouched and impenetrable.

Where are you?

I look back down at the water as it swirls around the pilings of the dock I'm standing on.

Are you somewhere down there? Are you floating toward the bay? Or are you far away from here? Locked in some monster's basement or buried in an unmarked and shallow grave?

I think about where we found her vehicle and what it could mean. I think about the seat being set back to accommodate a driver far taller than Carla.

Disposing of her vehicle where he did means he has something to hide and had to act fast.

Was what he did with Carla just as rushed? Was it unplanned, unexpected? Was his coverup just as impulsive and improvised? If so, why haven't we found her?

My line of thinking lets me know that whether I want to

admit it or not I believe someone has abducted or killed her—most likely the latter.

So I've just killed her. Didn't intend to. Didn't know I was going to. It just happened. What do I do? I have to act fast. What do I do? I burn her clothes and mine. Destroy any evidence linking me to her. I . . . I've got to get rid of her body. Do I throw it in the water? Weight it down with something or just toss it in and hope it floats far away or that a gator gets it?

Or do I look for a quick place to hide it? Where? Where would that be?

When I look up again, I see where that might be. Across the river at about a fifteen degree angle from where I'm standing on the Hayes's dock, there's a small access area to the thick jungle-like swamp on the other side.

Hoping I'm wrong, I jump into the boat nearest to me, untie it, crank the motor, and back away from the dock.

I'm not sure whose boat it is, and I don't want to take the time to find out or to ask to borrow it.

Crossing the nearly two-hundred yards wide river, I pray and beg and plead not to find what I think I'm going to.

When I reach the other side, I pull onto the bank and tie the boat to the wooden frame holding the large plastic culvert.

It has been three days, with lots of rainfall, but I still look for footprints in the mud.

There are a few deep boot prints—perhaps from a very heavy man or someone carrying a body.

I avoid them as I make my way up the incline to the top of the bank.

The path I take, the path the boot prints follow, runs along the large black plastic drainage pipe.

Both sides of the pipe are lined with trees, dense with undergrowth. The path of the pipe is the only clear way to quickly walk through this part of the swamp.

The smell hits me first.

I'm only about twenty feet or so in when I smell the smell that is like no other, the smell of despair, of decay, of death.

I don't have to go any farther to know what it is.

It could be an animal, but I know it's not.

It could be someone other than Carla, but I know it's not.

I could turn around now and go notify the others and never have to witness the horror that is somewhere close by, but I can't do that.

As much as I wish more than anything at this moment that Carla wasn't dead, as much as I don't want to see the condition of her body after three days in the swamp, I have to, and not only to be a witness or to be her person in this moment, but to give me my best chance at catching whoever did this to her.

Before moving on, I pause for a moment to prepare myself as much as possible, to make sure I'm not just a friend and father figure who cares deeply for her, but an investigator who needs to see the scene in a certain way.

I want to take some deep breaths, but because of the smell I am unable to.

I continue up the slight incline, following the drainage pipe and the deep boot prints.

In another ten feet or so I see one of the most disturbing and horrific sights I ever have.

There to the right of the path, hanging by a pair of jumper cables from the branch of a swamp tupelo tree is the naked, decomposing body of someone I had cared for and taken care of since she was sixteen years old.

CHAPTER
FORTY-EIGHT

I HAVE no doubt that it's her, but the body before me bears little resemblance to Carla.

Like most decomposing bodies I've seen, it bears little resemblance to any living person.

Her head is slumped over the jumper cables to the right, and her hair hangs down to cover part of her face. There's a foamy bloody substance in and around her nostrils.

Her body is bloated and has a greenish-purplish hue, the swollen veins beneath it pressing up to create marbling.

The lower parts of her legs and feet are a deep, dark purple-plum color from where gravity has caused her blood to settle there.

Her skin is blistered and slippage has begun.

Though insects have long since gotten to work on her body, surprisingly, mercifully, no scavengers have yet.

Having to see her without clothes, in such a sad vulnerable position, knowing the extinguishing of the flame of her life was neither peaceful nor pleasant would be bad enough, but to see her hanging from a tree after three days of decay and decomposition is disturbing and devastating beyond description, and something deep inside me breaks.

Trying to take as much in as possible, I study the scene and take pictures with my phone.

There's not much to go on.

It seems obvious that she wasn't killed here, and I doubt very much she was killed by hanging. That bit of staging is perhaps the biggest clue of all.

CHAPTER
FORTY-NINE

"I'M SORRY AS HELL," Fred Miller is saying.

"We all are," Michelle says.

Miller adds, "I was holding out hope that we'd get a better outcome. I know she was like . . . family to you. I'm just . . . so, so sorry."

Arnie Ward nods. "Anything we can do," he says. "Anything at all. Just let us know."

We are standing on the bank of the river near the drainage pipe, watching and waiting as FDLE processes the scene and the medical examiner's investigator processes Carla's body.

At the moment, I don't feel much of anything and feel as though I'm experiencing everything from a great distance away.

"You go on home and do what you need to do," Miller says. "We'll take care of everything here."

I shake my head. "I'm not leaving until she does. I have to be here with her."

"Okay," he says, nodding. "That's fine. But once you do go home, you take as much time as you need to—"

"I don't need any time," I say. "I need us to find who did this to her."

"We will. You have my word on that. Don't you worry."

"We will," Arnie says.

They both say it in a way that lets me know the "we" doesn't include me.

"Obviously, you can't work this case," he says, "so here's what I want you two to do. I want you to swap cases. Arnie, I want you taking over Carla's case. John, I want you taking over the Nelson woman's case. Y'all meet with each other and share everything and transfer the files and—"

"I've got to work Carla's case," I say.

"You can't," Miller says. "Even if you were able to—mentally and emotionally. Even if it was possible for you . . . You can't because we'd never get a conviction if you . . . A defense attorney would have the case thrown out before it even got started."

"I've got to work it," I say. "For her. For me. This is what I do, what I'm . . . there's no way I can't do this for her."

"I understand you wanting to," Miller says, "but it's just not possible. I know you don't want whoever did this to get away with it. And that's what would happen if you work on it."

"I have to work her case," I say. "I can do it as a private citizen if I have to."

"Whoa," Miller says. "Wait now. Don't throw your career away. Don't wreck your life. Don't—"

"I don't have a choice. I'm not trying to . . . It's not a . . . lack of trust in Arnie or anything else. It's just something I have to do. I've spent my life doing this. It's Carla. I have to do it for her."

"Give me a minute to . . ." Miller says.

I do.

He takes a few moments and appears to be thinking.

"I don't want to see you lose your job over this, and I don't want to lose you. Okay . . . How about this? Both of you work both cases. But Arnie is lead on Carla's case, and you are lead on Olivia Nelson. Okay? And I mean it. Arnie is lead on this case. You can help him. You can work it. But it's his case. He has to be included in everything. He'll be the one taking the case to court. Understand?"

I nod.

"I mean it, John," he says. "I'm going out on a limb on this for you. Doing you a huge favor. Don't make me regret it. Don't do anything to keep us from being able to get a conviction."

"I won't. And I really appreciate you allowing me to keep my job and work for her. You won't regret it."

CHAPTER
FIFTY

ALL I WANT to do is get home and be with my family and comfort John Paul, but I have to go to Rudy's to tell Carla's father first.

Rudy's is a small town diner on a rural highway outside of Pottersville.

It glows brightly against the dark night on the side of the empty highway.

I pull into the parking lot, remembering how many times I had done so before—nearly all of them with Carla waiting inside, wanting to talk, needing to sleep.

Allegedly open twenty-four hours, every light is on and the door is unlocked, but no one is inside, and it's a safe bet that Rudy is passed out in the back.

Since Carla stopped covering the overnight shift, Rudy's had not really been open much beyond an early dinner hour.

The cold, brightly lit diner feels creepy and abandoned, especially when, randomly, the jukebox comes to life and begins to play.

As if the universe is mocking me, the song that begins to play is "How to Save a Life" by The Fray.

As the familiar piano notes start, I quickly make my way through the diner to the back.

I find Rudy passed out in a lonely old recliner in front of a TV playing a black and white western with the sound turned down.

Next to the recliner is a nearly empty bottle of gin.

"Rudy," I say.

He doesn't stir.

"Rudy," I say more loudly and shake his shoulder.

"Huh? What? What is it?"

He blinks several times, but when he sees that it's me his eyes open wide and he jerks up.

"She's dead, isn't she?" he says.

I nod. "I'm sorry."

"Where? How?"

"Don't have a lot of details yet," I say. "I wanted to come let you know as soon as possible."

"Where did y'all find her?"

"On the river."

"Drowned?"

"We don't know the cause of death yet," I say, "but I don't think she drowned."

"Was she . . . Did someone kill her?"

"It'd be speculating—"

"Then speculate, goddamnit. I know you know more than you're tellin' me."

"I honestly don't know much yet, but it's definitely a suspicious death. I'll let you know more when we do."

"My little girl," he says, starting to cry.

"I'm very sorry."

"She always thought you were such hot shit. Good guy. Super cop. You couldn't even protect her. Couldn't even keep her alive. What kind of super cop are you? You've got her and everybody else fooled, don't you? You're nothing. A fuckin' fraud. That's all you are. Couldn't even protect my little girl. Why'd you take her away from me if you weren't goin' to take care of her? Get out of here, you worthless . . . son of a bitch. You . . . And don't you dare think you're going to . . . You took my daughter away from me. You're not going to get my grandson. I promise you that."

As I walk through the diner, Springsteen's "The River" is playing and it continues to play in my head long after I can no longer hear the old juke box playing it in the empty roadside establishment that is now haunted for me.

CHAPTER
FIFTY-ONE

ANNA MEETS me in the driveway, tears streaming out of her red eyes and down her cry-swollen cheeks.

Wordlessly we hold each other, grieving beneath a waning moon out of view of the children.

For the first time since I had found Carla, I let myself really feel the loss, the tragedy, the horror.

Safe in Anna's arms and away from the rest of the world, the dam inside me breaks and I begin to sob, grief pouring out of me in deep, gut-wrenching waves.

Part of me is grieving for Reggie too, and all of me is grieving for John Paul, a little boy who we have to give the worst news imaginable to in a few minutes.

Right now John Paul is inside our home playing, having fun, with no idea that his little world has already been irrevocably altered, utterly and completely changed forever.

After I few moments, I begin to pull it together.

For now I've indulged my grief enough. I have two missions that require all of my focus and attention, that demand I be clear-headed and locked in—taking care of John Paul and figuring out who took his mother from him.

As we enter our home, this safe haven and sanctuary, I think about the two other children who live here who have experienced similar losses. Taylor lost her father before ever getting to know him, and Nash is with us because his mom was murdered. We had helped them deal with their devastating losses, and we will help John Paul deal with his. And I suspect they will help him too.

We gather the family into the living room.

Detecting our mood and manner, seeing that we have been crying, they are instantly quiet and somber.

All four kids are on the couch, and Anna and I are kneeling on the floor in front of them.

Nash is on the left end, then John Paul, Taylor, and Johanna. They are all touching each other. Nash has his arm around John Paul. Taylor is holding hands with him and Johanna.

They're preparing themselves. They know what's coming.

"We love you all so much," I say. "And we always will. We will take care of you and protect you. You can always count on us. Always."

Anna nods. "We are a family. All of us. Each of you are part of this very special and loving family."

"There's nothing we can't get through together, nothing we can't help each other deal with."

"I am here for you. I'm not going anywhere. Anna is here for you. She's not going anywhere. And y'all have each other. And always will."

I look at John Paul. "I love you so much, little buddy. And I'm so, so sorry. But we just found out that your mommy has gone to heaven."

He breaks down and starts crying, and soon we all are.

"She didn't want to go," I say. "She didn't want to leave you. Some bad person made her do it. She never ever would have left you if it was up to her, but it wasn't. A very bad person took her from us."

"Mommy," he cries. "I want my mommy."

Everyone moves in and gathers around John Paul, all of us in a kind of group hug with John Paul in the center, all of us crying with him, consoling him and each other.

"My mommy's dead," John Paul says in a tearful moan. "I miss my mommy. I want her back."

I'm so proud of how the other kids are responding to John Paul and his devastating sorrow, and I can tell for Nash part of what he's doing is grieving the loss of his own mom. His experience of loss has given him the ability to practice compassion and empathy on a profound level, particularly for what John Paul is going through.

I lean over and hug him extra tight. "So proud of you," I whisper.

"Mommy," John Paul wails again. "I want my mommy."

CHAPTER
FIFTY-TWO

THAT NIGHT we sleep as a family on the floor of the living room with John Paul in the center.

Once everyone is asleep and I know they are okay, I ease up and slip out of the house.

Driving to Carla's, I glance at my phone and see I've missed calls from Dad, Merrill, Sam, Daniel, Merrick, Arnie, Michelle, Fred Miller, Darlene, and Hank Stevens.

As I search Carla's place again, I listen to the messages and read over the texts.

The first search I did of Carla's small apartment was a quick search for any obvious signs of violence or clues to where she might have been. Now that I know her fate, I'm doing a much more thorough search.

Knowing that she'll never have even another second of breath, of life, of growing and evolving, maturing, and pursuing her dreams, makes this small, cluttered, dirty apartment all the more sad and tragic.

Wearing gloves and trying to disturb everything as little as possible, I start in her bedroom.

Her unmade bed has two pillows and two obvious spots where people have slept recently—one adult size and one the size of a small child. Most nights even if John Paul started in his big boy bed he'd wind up in here with his mommy, something he'll never get to do again.

I blink my stinging eyes and look away.

Searching through her closet, drawers, bedside table, beneath her bed, I place my phone on top of her dresser and play the messages on speaker.

"John, Hank Stevens here. I want to extend my condolences to you from my family. I'm very sorry for your loss. Carla had a lot of potential and was a good girl. I'd like to meet with you at your earliest convenience to discuss a few things, including how my office can assist you in the investigation. I know you spoke with Easton earlier. I just want to reiterate that he had nothing to do with any of this, obviously. I won't have his life turned upside down or he or his wife embarrassed because . . . Look, I know you're going to be gunning for revenge. I get it. I want to help you catch the bastard who did this. But don't let your anger and sorrow make you hurt innocent people. Okay? That's the main thing. Don't punish innocent people just because you're upset. Call me when you can."

"I'm so sorry, son," Dad says. "Call me when you can. Let me know what Verna and I can do. And anything my office can do just let me know. Anything at all."

Merrill's message says, "I'm here. Anything you need. Call me."

Besides more sadness and deep sorrow, the only thing I turn up in Carla's bedroom is a journal in between her mattress and boxsprings near the top of her bed by her nightstand.

I bag it to bring with me.

Though I don't expect to find anything of evidentiary value, I search John Paul's room.

Setting down the evidence bags in the hallway, I open a large trash bag and fill it with the toys and stuffed animals I think will be the most comforting. I also grab his pillow, blanket, and the picture of him and his mom on his little nightstand.

The living room and kitchen don't yield anything helpful, but the bathroom delivers a bombshell.

In the bottom of the small trash can, beneath wadded tissues, Q-tips, and a few empty makeup and hygiene containers, I find a positive pregnancy test.

CHAPTER
FIFTY-THREE

BACK IN MY TRUCK, I call Zaire, Merrill's wife.

She's a doctor at Sacred Heart in Port St. Joe, and I have a few questions for her.

Merrill answers.

"Just about to come looking for you," he says.

"Spent the evening with the family, comforting John Paul," I say. "Just got them to sleep not long ago."

"Where you now?" he asks.

"In my truck outside Carla's apartment. Got a couple of questions for Za."

"Ask away," he says. "You on speaker."

"Hey, John," she says. "I'm so, so sorry about Carla. Let us know anything we can do to help."

"Thank you."

Someone pulls into the apartment complex, their headlights hitting my rearview.

"I just found a pregnancy test in Carla's apartment," I say. "I have no idea when she took it, but she's been missing three days so . . . at least that long. Will the reading still be accurate?"

"Depends," she says. "A negative reading is probably still

accurate. If it reads positive it's going to depend on a few factors."

"I thought I had heard somewhere that negative results can flip positive over time," I say.

"That's right," she says. "It can happen—especially with the cheap tests. What's being tested is the woman's HCG hormone. It needs to be a five or greater. It doubles every forty-eight hours, so the farther along she is the better chance for an accurate result is. The more distinct the positive line will be and the better chance it's not a negative test that flipped positive later. How thick and dark and distinct is the positive line?"

"Very," I say.

"Then the chances are very good that she was actually pregnant—and probably a few months."

Merrill says, "And chances are there's the motive for her murder."

CHAPTER
FIFTY-FOUR

"CARLA WAS PREGNANT," I whisper.

We are sitting at our kitchen table having a quiet cup of tea, the kids a few feet away asleep on the floor in the living room.

Anna frowns, tears glistening in her eyes.

It was one of our fears. Carla was having a difficult enough time taking care of John Paul—even with our help. We wondered what she'd do if she had another child. We wondered what we'd do. Now I wish we would've been able to find out.

"Seems more of a motive for Easton than Mason," she says.

I nod. "Yes, it does. Or Easton's wife. But it may not have been part of the motive at all. We've got to find out whose it was and who if anyone even knew about it."

She nods. "Yeah, hard to see that really being the motive."

"Certainly not what it once was, is it? But . . . it could've been part of what caused someone to lose it in the moment. Not necessarily the motive behind a premeditated murder."

"That what you think happened?"

I shrug and nod. "Seems to be spur of the moment, unplanned, disorganized."

She shakes her head, more tears spilling out of her eyes. "Still can't believe she's gone."

I nod and take her hand, trying not to think about it.

On the way back home I had called Michelle and told her what I had discovered and asked her to get the ME to check to confirm and take the necessary steps for us to be able to do paternity tests. I also asked her to keep it quiet for now.

"We are going to take John Paul in, aren't we?" she asks.

I nod.

"Think anyone will fight us for him?"

I shrug. "I've given up guessing what other people will do, but . . . it's hard to imagine anyone will . . . His biological father has never had anything to do with him, and on Carla's side there's only Rudy."

I don't tell her any of what Rudy said.

"Don't suppose she ever made a will," she says.

Anna had encouraged her to make a will after John Paul was born and even offered to help her, but as far as we know she never did it.

"Her bedside table seemed to hold all her important papers," I say. "I bagged them and brought them with me, but I haven't looked through them yet."

"I can't see Mason or Easton agreeing to a paternity test," she says. "Especially Easton."

I nod.

There are ways around that, but I don't mention it.

"Mason might be willing, but . . ." she says. "I doubt it. No upside. He'll still be the prime suspect whether it's his or Easton's. If her death has something to do with her pregnancy or who she was involved with—and they most often do—who else has a motive? Mason and Easton. Easton's wife, Meg, right? Lillian Mosely, who Mason was still seeing . . ."

"Lily's husband, Joel," I say. "He could've gone out there looking for Mason and found Carla instead and got into an altercation and . . ."

"True."

Eventually, we lay back down on the living room floor with the kids.

Anna is asleep in moments.

And with my family sleeping around me, I open Carla's diary with gloved hands and read her most intimate thoughts and feelings in the light from my phone as "The River" echoes in my head.

CHAPTER
FIFTY-FIVE

JORDAN GRANT IS a late-twenties single mom of twin boys who works at one of the three Dollar Stores in town.

She's biracial with the most exquisite toffee skin, big black eyes, and long black hair.

I catch her on a break, eating a Honey Bun and drinking a Diet Mountain Dew on the side of the corrugated tin building.

"I still can't believe she's really gone," she says with tears in her eyes. "We weren't all that close, but . . ."

"She wrote in her diary what a good friend you were to her," I say.

Carla only wrote in her diary occasionally, sporadically, and mostly about John Paul. I'm working my way through it, searching for clues as to what happened to her and who might be responsible, but I'm not hopeful there will be much in it that's helpful in that regard.

She nods. "I was."

"But you two weren't close?"

"Right. I was a good friend to her when she'd let me be. She wasn't really a good friend to me. She wasn't bad to me or anything. It was sort of one-sided and only like . . . here and there . . . now and then. She had y'all. She depended on y'all. She ran with Bailey some, but mostly if she was taking time away from John Paul it was to be with a guy."

"Who all was she seeing?"

"Mason Hayes," she says. "Before him. Easton. Before that . . . nobody in particular. A random hookup here and there."

Jordan was Carla's most settled friend, the one she could count on for help with John Paul, support, and sound advice.

"We never went out together or anything," she says. "I don't really go out. Don't date. I take care of my boys and work. That's about all I have time for. She'd come over and hang out some while the boys played. She'd get me to keep John Paul some. But that was about it. We'd talk a little when she'd bring him by or pick him up or when she'd hang a little, but that's about it."

"Did you know she was pregnant?"

She nods. "She asked me what I thought she should do. I was honest with her. I told her it seemed like she was having a hard enough time caring for JP, so if she *did* keep it she needed to get serious about making motherhood more of a priority. Don't get me wrong. She wasn't a bad mother. She was good. But her focus was scattered some. You can't really be about your kids *and* chasing a guy."

"Did she know whose it was?" I ask.

She shakes her head. "Said she wasn't sure. She . . . I think she and Easton still slipped off occasionally and she must've gotten pregnant around the time she was seeing both him and Mason. But I don't know for sure."

"Did she say whether she was going to keep it or not?" I ask.

"Didn't say. Just asked my advice. Talked about how she felt. And—"

"How'd she feel?"

"Torn. She wanted it but knew she didn't have the bandwidth for it."

"Do you know who all she had told?" I ask. "Had she told Mason and Easton?"

"I don't think she'd told anyone else at that point. But that was about a week ago, so . . . She was dreading tellin' you. Said she knew you'd be understanding and want to help, but she felt guilty, like y'all had helped her so much with John Paul and she had gone and gotten pregnant again without being in a stable relationship. And it may have even been by someone who was married to someone else."

"Who do you think killed her?" I ask.

She shakes her head. "I have no idea. I can't see either Mason or Easton doing it. I mean, I guess chances are it was one of them, right? But neither seems the type. I don't know. Maybe it was someone she didn't even know and didn't have anything to do with, and she was in the wrong place at the wrong time. That's what I'm hoping for."

CHAPTER
FIFTY-SIX

"VERY PRELIMINARY AUTOPSY results are somewhat inconclusive," Michelle is saying.

She has joined me, Arnie, and Darlene in Fred Miller's office.

"Inconclusive?" Miller says.

"So far. Doesn't mean they'll end up that way."

"But inconclusive between what?" he says.

"Manner and cause of death," she says. "Whether it was homicide or suicide. Typically in a hanging the rope rides up on the neck in the shape of an inverted V. With strangulation, the rope marks around the neck are more level. Obviously, if strangulation was caused by hands then thumb and finger marks will often appear. A hanged neck is usually more damaged than a strangled neck. I'm talking about on an actual hanging. With an actual hanging the neck might be broken, or even stretched, but this isn't a hanging. This is a strangulation. A hanging requires a drop to break the neck. This is a strangulation. The question is . . . did the victim do it herself or was it done to her. Suicide by self strangulation is only second to firearms, but homicide by hanging is extremely rare."

"All of that's true," I say, "but . . . there's a third option."

She nods.

"Which is what?" Darlene asks.

"That she was strangled to death and then hung up in an attempt to cover it up."

"Right," Michelle says. "A strangled body will generally have petechiae and other marks in the face and eyes that a hanging doesn't. Death by hanging shuts down blood in both directions, so there are usually fewer symptoms. The thing is . . . the condition of the body . . . given that it had been hanging out there in the elements for three days . . . is making it difficult to determine certain aspects of manner and cause of death with absolute certainty. We'll eventually get a determination. They just wanted us to know where things stand in these early stages."

"I think it's a suicide," Darlene says. "I think she was devastated to be left like that. Humiliated. But she didn't want to do it right there where everybody would see, so she broke into the storage locker, grabbed the cables, swam across the river, and hung herself."

"It wasn't suicide," I say.

"I think it was," she says. "You're too close to see it, but . . . and with her being pregnant and desperate and rejected."

I glare at Michelle.

"It wasn't suicide," I say. "And her being pregnant supports that. No way she'd kill herself. She wouldn't leave John Paul, and she wouldn't do it over being pregnant."

"Everybody who kills themselves leaves people behind," Darlene says. "Children. Parents. Spouses. And everybody always thinks their loved one didn't kill themselves, that they couldn't."

"We're gonna follow the evidence," Miller says. "No matter where it leads us."

"The evidence says it wasn't suicide," I say. "She didn't have her clothes on and they weren't found at the scene."

"Mason could've taken them," she says. "Would've made her more embarrassed and desperate. He fucks her, then leaves her naked and alone."

I shake my head. "It's very likely her clothes were burned in the fire at the McDaniel place. That's someone covering up a crime, destroying evidence. The rubber found in the fire is probably from the boots that made the prints found at the crime scene."

"Someone could've come along and stolen her clothes and things," she says. "After she was already dead. Her phone. Her jewelry. Her clothes. They could've left the bootprints."

"Then there would've been footprints from where she walked up there to begin with. And you'd have to ignore the fire at the McDaniel's. *And* . . . I don't think she could've swum across the river naked carrying jumper cables, but even if she could . . . the current would've taken her a lot farther downstream. And none of this takes into account that her car was hidden, driven into the river. That was done by whoever killed her. She didn't do it. No one else had a motive or would've had her keys."

"You just don't want to see the truth,"

"That's all I want to see," I say. "And everything *I've* said is based on the evidence. You have to ignore evidence for your theory to work."

"Continue to investigate," Miller says. "Follow the evidence. And for now keep her being pregnant to ourselves. Everybody keep an open mind and go where the evidence leads. Nowhere else."

Arnie says, "We gonna ask Mason and Easton to take paternity tests?"

Miller nods. "Eventually. But we can't make them, so we have to wait for the right time and frame it the right way. Hopefully we'll get more helpful evidence back from FDLE and the ME's office soon. Don't jump to conclusions. Wait to see what they say. Okay . . . Where are we with Olivia Nelson?"

"Her ex has a credible alibi for the night she was attacked," I say.

"Doesn't mean he wasn't involved," Darlene says.

"No, it doesn't. He could've hired someone to make himself look less suspicious."

"I think that's what he did," Darlene says. "He's gaslighting the shit out of her, preying on her vulnerabilities. Look at him hard."

"We are," I say.

Arnie says, "There's nothing helpful from her attack. No prints. No DNA. No physical evidence of any kind."

"Another suspect we need to consider is Easton Stevens," I say. "He's already a suspect in Carla's murder. I think he could have something to do with what's happening to Olivia Nelson also. He was out in the wooded lot the night we found Roy. Claims he saw the light and went to check it out, but he didn't call 9-1-1 and he left the scene without identifying himself or even letting us know he was there. He also hit me on the back of the head before leaving."

"Okay, let's look at him closely, but . . . follow the evidence. Nothing else. Don't force things to fit theories of who you want to be guilty."

"I've been keeping a close eye on Olivia," Darlene says. "Watching over her most nights."

I look over at her. That's an odd way to phrase that.

"But I've been thinking," she goes on to say, "the guy sees my car there he's probably not going to try anything, so . . . I'm gonna start parking it somewhere else and see if he comes back."

"Radio us the moment anything happens," Miller says.

"Where will you be set up if your car is not there?" I ask.

"Inside," she says. "He breaks in again, I got something for his creepy ass."

CHAPTER
FIFTY-SEVEN

THE NORTHROP SISTERS, Cinda and Lucinda, are rough, outdoorsy, middle-aged women with sunbaked skin and long wispy blond-going-gray hair.

They're from South Georgia but have a river camp here they spend as much time at as they can.

"We love it here," Cinda is saying. "Probably live here full-time when we retire."

"Fishin' is our all-time favorite pastime," Lucinda says.

Though not twins, they look like they could be, and I can't tell them apart.

"We remember the young man you're talkin' about," Cinda says. "He was cute. Lucinda likes 'em young."

"God help me, I do," Lucinda says.

"She waved to him and was gonna go over and talk to him, but he was in a state."

"What kind of state?"

"Just like irritated, frustrated. You could tell he was ready to get out of there. And that's what he did. Loaded up his boat and got out of there."

"He did," Lucinda says, "but he did stop by that car and put something on it."

"What car?" I ask.

"A little gray one," Cinda says. "Camry I think."

"It was," Lucinda says, nodding. "Had one of those stickers with initials on it and a dent in the bumper."

"What did he put on it?"

"Couldn't see exactly. Had to be small."

"Any idea what time this was?" I ask.

"Can tell you almost exactly," Cinda says. "I called my daughter when we got back to the landing and had signal."

She pulls out her phone and begins to scroll through the call log.

"She sent me a picture of my grandson too. Let's see . . . A few minutes after five."

"And he left and took his boat and didn't do anything else to the car? Didn't move it? Didn't drive it away?"

"Just lit out of there like a house on fire," Cinda says.

"And broke my heart a little," Lucinda says.

When the Northrop sisters have gone, Arnie and I remain in the interview room.

"It's lookin' less and less like he could've done it," Arnie says. "Such a narrow window. Based on the security camera footage from his parents' place, he didn't even leave his house until four."

I nod. "So by the time he gets to the end of the road, talks to Carla, drives to Tupelo Creek, launches his boat, goes down river to the cabin . . . He's probably only out there about half an hour. No wonder Carla felt used and didn't want to leave."

"It's so sad," he says. "I feel so bad for her."

"It's possible he could've killed her and taken her body over and hung it where we found it, but . . . it's hard to see him doing all that in half an hour. And the fact that he comes off the river when he does and is seen by the Northrop sisters and the fact that the Hayes's security system shows him coming home right after that and never leaving again means he couldn't have been the one who moved her car or set the fire at the McDaniels's."

"Yeah," he says.

"So we don't rule him out," I say, "but we move him down the list a little."

CHAPTER
FIFTY-EIGHT

"IT COULD BE EITHER ONE," Rhonda Suber is saying.

I'm back at the drive-thru at Good Spirits, this time with two photos, one of Meg Stevens and one of Lillian Mosely, both taken from the back.

"Really?" I ask.

"Yeah."

"But they . . . their sizes and shapes are nothing alike."

Meg Stevens has a tight, lean runner's body and blond hair. Lilian Mosely is shorter and thicker and has brown hair.

"She was leaning in toward Carla," she says, "so I couldn't tell how tall she was. And it was quite a ways away."

"Close your eyes and think back to what you saw. Try to picture it in your mind."

"Okay," she says, closing her eyes.

"What color was the woman's hair?"

"She was wearing a big yellow raincoat," she says. "That's why I can't tell how how big she was or what color her hair was."

"Was it raining?"

She opens her eyes as she shakes her head. "No, but it had been. Florida in August. Am I right?"

. . .

I drive straight to the school hoping to catch Lily Mosely before she leaves.

I find her in the parking lot near her car.

Not surprisingly, her vehicle is a lime-green VW Bug.

She is carrying a purse, a shoulder bag, a soft-cloth lunchbox, and wooden crate of art projects.

"Here," I say, grabbing the crate, "let me help you."

She opens her creaky car door, which isn't locked, and we place everything inside.

"Thanks," she says.

I take a step back, and she turns to face me, standing in the V created by the open door.

"Just need to talk to you for a few more minutes," I say.

"I heard about Carla," she says, shaking her head. "I'm . . . so, so sorry. My heart absolutely breaks for that poor little boy. I'm . . . I'm so glad he has you and Anna."

She looks tired—and not just from a day of herding cats in the form of kindergartners. Her thick brown hair is pulled up in a ponytail, but wisps of it have escaped and float around in the breeze, and her brown eyes seem smaller and not as bright as before—and they have dark half-moons beneath them.

"Did you and Carla get into an altercation?" I ask.

She looks equal parts hurt and shocked. "No. I . . . I don't get into altercations. I'm . . . I would never. No."

"We have a witness who says she saw you and Carla arguing."

"Well, they're mistaken. It wasn't me. I wouldn't. I couldn't. Over what? Mason? I wish I had never been so stupid as to . . . do what I did. I certainly don't want him back or . . . I'd have nothing whatsoever to argue with Carla about."

She stops talking and pastes a pleasant expression on her face as another teacher walks out and gets into her vehicle nearby.

"Do you have a raincoat?" I ask when the other teacher is gone.

She nods.

"What color is it?"

"I have a few. Let's see . . . a pink one with white polkadots. A white one with pink polkadots. One with little dinosaurs. One with kittens. One with—"

"Do you have a yellow one?"

She nods.

"Were you wearing it on Sunday?"

She shrugs. "Could'a been. Don't remember."

"Did you go to the end of the road, the landing, or Gaskin Park that day?"

"I probably did," she says. "I live on Byrd Parker not far from there, and that's where I walk my dogs."

"Did you see Carla there?"

She shakes her head. "No. Certainly not to talk to. I would tell you."

"What did you do after you came off the river with Mason?" I ask.

She looks up and narrows her eyes as if searching her memory.

"I went home and took the longest, hottest shower I could. Actually ran out of hot water I stayed in so long trying to wash my sin off me. Then I got in the bed and cried myself to sleep. When I woke up I took the dogs for a walk. When I got back I took a long bubble bath. I then did an online counseling session. Then I ate two half gallons of pistachio ice cream. Cried some more. Watched some bad reruns. Reread some passages from Anna Karenina and the Scarlet Letter. Avoided Joel. Pretended to be asleep when he got home. Eventually fell asleep."

"What time did he get home?"

"Eight or nine maybe. Not sure."

"Okay. Thank you for your time."

"I feel so guilty," she says. "I'm so ashamed of what I did."

"Regret and remorse for mistakes are good," I say, "but only when we face what we did, learn from it, and commit to doing better and not repeating an unhealthy cycle. Don't get mired in guilt. Feel remorse. Learn your lessons. Let it go. Forgive yourself. Move on."

"It's one thing to do what I did, but to do it to Joel. To betray him like that."

"Have you spoken to him about it yet?"

She shakes her head. "I haven't. I'm not going to. I can't. Do you think I should?"

"I do," I say. "Unless you feel it's unsafe to do so."

"It will devastate him. But he won't . . . He's not the type of man to hit me or do anything violent."

"Then you should tell him."

"He'll never forgive me. It will end us."

"He might surprise you," I say, "but either way . . . he should be told and get to decide. You've already betrayed him. Don't keep the betrayal going and make it worse by not telling him."

CHAPTER
FIFTY-NINE

I FIND Meg Stevens running on Old Dairy Farm Road near a grove of pecan trees.

I pull onto the twin trail dirt road beneath the trees, the pecan shells crunching under my tires, and she jogs over to my truck.

The trees are spaced far apart and provide little shade from the slanting late afternoon sun, and brittle, brown leaves crackle beneath our shoes.

Meg's pale-blue running attire is new and stylish and tight enough to serve as a second skin. Her blond hair is pulled back into a ponytail that swishes around as she moves, and her eyes are hidden behind dark shades.

As she reaches me, she pulls out her Air Buds and wipes the sweat on her forehead with her forearm.

"Sorry to interrupt your run," I say.

"No problem. I've already done more than I planned on. Just heading back home now."

In the reflection of her shades, my head looks big and distorted.

"This about Olivia Nelson's stalker?" she asks.

"Not unless you have anything new to add."

"Not really. But I have noticed a vehicle cruising around our neighborhood the last two nights—a large, dark car. Like an older model, I guess."

"We'll check it out," I say. "Anything else."

"I guess not. Just feel bad for her. She seems like a really unhappy woman and then to have to deal with all this. I don't know . . . it's just . . . sad."

"Do you have a yellow raincoat?" I ask.

She looks confused. "Ah . . . yeah. Why?"

"I have a witness who says they saw you arguing with Carla Pearson on the day she disappeared."

Her brow furrows, and she shakes her head like a bee is buzzing around it.

"Who said *that*?" she asks.

"Is it true?"

"I have a right to know who's accusing me."

"Did you have words with Carla on Sunday afternoon?" I ask.

"I . . . I certainly didn't . . . argue or fight with her or anyone else. I may have spoken to her."

"At the end of the road?"

She nods slowly.

"What did you say to her?"

"It's private."

"There's nothing private in a murder investigation."

"But it has nothing to do with that."

"We can't just take your word for that," I say.

"Oh my God, I can't believe I'm . . . Why did I . . . The timing. How could I have been so stupid?"

"How stupid were you?" I ask.

"I just meant . . . I shouldn't've said anything. It was so stupid and high school-ish. And to do it on the day she went missing . . . I swear I have the worst luck in the world."

"I'd say Carla might have you beat."

"Well, yeah. Yes, of course. It was just an expression. I'm . . . I didn't mean."

"What did you say to her?"

"I just asked her if she was seeing my husband," she says. "They used to be an item before he and I—Well, I'm sure you know. Anyway, I suspected her of trying to get him back, and I was stupid enough to ask her."

"How'd you know where she'd be?" I ask. "What were you doing at the landing?"

"I . . . I can track Easton on my phone. He had been there earlier. I think I just missed him, but when I saw her . . . It like confirmed my greatest fears. I . . . I just asked her if she was seeing my husband and—"

"What did she say?"

"Not much. I didn't give her time to say much. She . . . she just . . . I remember her shaking her head and tears filling her eyes. I told her I was pregnant and we were starting a family and Easton needed to be a father to his child and a faithful husband to his child's mother. I was upset. I was . . . I didn't really listen or give her a chance to respond. I just sort of spewed all that on her and left. I feel bad. But I was just trying to protect my family. Anyone would. It was probably my hormones. But I didn't touch her. And I didn't do anything to her. And I didn't have anything to do with what happened to her."

"What did Easton say about the confrontation?"

"I didn't tell him. He doesn't know about it."

"Just because you didn't tell him doesn't mean he didn't know about it."

"He doesn't know about it. He would've said something. We tell each other everything."

I try to suppress my reaction to that.

"Everything that matters anyway."

"Does Easton sleep around?"

She has the look of a trapped animal. She has just told me they tell each other everything.

New beads of sweat begin to pop out on her face and fore-head, small bubbles of which line her upper lip.

She gives me a little shrug. "Like all men, he strays from time to time."

I don't point out to her that not all men do. That's not the conversation I'm here to have.

"With Carla?"

"They . . . You know how it is . . . I think Easton and I got together before they were . . . completely over. They had unfinished business. But we didn't have anything to do with what happened to her."

"Who else has he . . . *strayed* with?"

She shrugs. "I don't . . . get play by play. But the fact that it wasn't just Carla lets you know he wasn't hung up on her. Neither of us were. We weren't obsessed or . . . We had no reason to harm her. He just likes a lot of sex and a lot of variety. Like all men."

"Who else?"

"I'm not gonna give you a list . . . I think he fucked one of Carla's friends to prove to her she wasn't special. And he had a brief thing with Olivia Nelson when she first moved here. So see Carla wasn't . . . I don't mean she wasn't . . . special . . . I mean we didn't kill her. We had no reason to. None whatsoever."

CHAPTER
SIXTY

"JOHN MOTHERFUCKER JORDAN," Bailey Bozeman says when I walk up.

She's sitting on the tailgate of her old beater truck, which she has backed up to the edge of the Dead Lakes at the foot of the old dam.

"Startin' to think maybe you got a little thing for me," she says. "You're stalkery as fuck."

She has a bottle of Bud Light in her left hand and is skimming rocks off the surface of the water with her right. In between she swings her dangling legs like a small child would do.

"How are you?" I ask.

She shrugs. "Same as usual. A'right, I reckon. Sort of my default setting. Never let myself get too high or too low. 'Course too high is not usually the problem. Life has pretty much always been a bitch to me. But I ain't gonna let the old bitch get me down, you know? Just keep movin'. Keep givin' her the finger."

That must explain why she's not too broken up about Carla.

"You're not fishing?" I say.

She shakes her head. "Just hangin'."

Often between jobs and with no real interests, Bailey spends a lot of time just hangin'.

"Thinkin' a lot about Carla," she says. "Miss that hooker. Hey, let's pour out a toast offering to her."

She turns to the small plastic cooler next to her, pulls out a bottle of Bud Light, and hands it to me.

I twist off the cap and put it in my pocket, a little curl of smoke rising up from the mouth of the dark bottle.

We hold up our bottles.

"To Carla," I say.

"To Carla," she repeats. "I miss the shit out of you, bitch."

We then pour out the contents of our drinks onto the ground.

We are quiet a moment, and I can feel the soul-crushing weight of guilt and grief pressing down on me.

"Still can't believe she's gone," she says.

I nod.

She goes back into her cooler for another bottle and offers me one.

"I'm good, thanks."

"Thank Christ Almighty," she says. "Already wasted two good beers to the ground. You'd'a broken my teeny tiny little heart if you'd'a said yes."

"Answer a few questions and I'll buy your next six pack."

"It was a suitcase," she says.

"Okay. Your next suitcase."

"Bet," she says. "Fire away."

"What's the talk around town?" I ask.

"So far it's just small town gossip and bullshit," she says. "Strange theories and pointing fingers at innocent people, including you."

"Me?"

"Yeah. Said y'all were too close for you not to be fuckin' her. You do too much for John Paul for him not to be your son—and his name proves it. Say she was seein' other guys and in a jealous rage you killed her. Or Anna finally had enough and she did it. And since you're a cop and workin' the actual fuckin' investigation you can cover the whole thing up."

"Wow," I say. I wasn't expecting that.

"No good deed, am I right?"

"So you don't believe it?"

"'Course not. You're one of the good guys. Anybody with any sense knows that. Plus, Carla confided in me. I know what's what and who's who."

"What else is bein' said?"

"Mostly bullshit like that. Most everyone suspects Mason Hayes. Not many know she was still seein' Easton, but those that do suspect him. Me, personally, I can't see either of them havin' the balls for something like this."

"Anything else?"

"Not really."

"Wasn't really worth a suitcase, was it?"

"Someone said that Easton slept with one of Carla's friends to hurt her. Was that you?"

She laughs loudly. "I'm flattered, but . . . Easton likes 'em skinny. I'm way too much woman for him."

"I'm not sure his type would enter into it if he was just trying to hurt Carla."

"Well, the sadistic bastard didn't try to hurt her with me," she says. "I changed teams a few years back. Sports too. I've been more of a softballer these days."

She grabs the top of her bottle with her left hand and releases her right so I can see the koozie beneath it.

It's a cat with its mouth wide open, its hair standing up, and an alarmed expression on its face with the caption, "Lesbians eat WHAT????"

I smile. "Cute."

"So, it ain't me, babe," she says in her best Dylan. "It ain't me you're lookin' for."

"Any idea who it might be?" I ask.

"No, but I'll find out."

CHAPTER
SIXTY-ONE

DARLENE WEATHERLY OPENS Olivia Nelson's door with her gun drawn.

She's in casual attire and sock feet and looks like she has moved in.

"Told you I'd have somethin' for the bastard when he comes back," she says, holstering her weapon on her right hip.

"Yes, you did," I say insincerely. "Is Olivia home? Can you ask her to step out here for a moment?"

"Come on in," she says. "I'm cookin' dinner."

"You go finish that up," I say. "This won't take but a minute. Just ask her to step out here."

"Suit yourself," she says with a half shrug and disappears back into the house.

A few minutes later, Olivia Nelson appears at the door—at least I think it's Olivia Nelson. She has changed so much it's hard to tell.

No longer the worried, anxious, frightened, sleep-deprived mess she was, she appears relaxed and rested and lighter.

"Would you mind stepping out here a moment?" I ask.

She steps onto the porch with me, and I pull the door closed behind her. I don't want Darlene to hear our conversation.

"How are you?" I ask. "You seem—"

"So much better," she says. "Darlene has saved my life. I'm sleeping and eating again. She's . . . amazing. I feel so safe with her here."

"I'm so glad to see you doing so well," I say.

"It's wonderful, isn't it? I feel like a new woman."

"That's great," I say.

"Would you like to stay for dinner?" she asks.

"Thank you, but I can't. I just have a couple of questions for you and I'll let you get back to it."

"Okay."

"Are you or were you involved with Easton Stevens?"

She frowns and drops her head. Eventually, she nods slowly. "I was," she says. "Not any more. It was brief and stupid and ended a long time ago. It was barely anything, but . . . I was new here, and he was so welcoming and helpful and . . . but as I say it ended about the time it started and that was when I first moved here. Please don't say anything. I don't know who told you, but . . . I really don't want it to get out. It was a huge mistake, and we both agreed to act as if it never happened."

"Could he be the one who's harassing you?" I ask.

"No," she says too quickly and without conviction. "It's not him."

"His wife?" I ask.

"No. Absolutely not. They aren't that kind of people."

"I don't feel like you're tellin' me the truth," I say.

"Well, I am. May I go back inside now?"

"Does he frighten you?"

She steps closer to me, leans in, and whispers. "They live right there. They can see everything that goes on here. His dad's a powerful man. Drop it. Leave them out of it. You'll only make things worse for me if you don't."

CHAPTER
SIXTY-TWO

WHEN I GET HOME, I find Anna on the back patio.

She's stretched out in a lounge chair with a glass of red wine.

I sit beside her and take her hand.

Silently, we gaze at the spectacular sunset before us.

The sun has already ducked beneath the horizon, leaving behind a pumpkin-colored glow that backlights the cypress trees rimming Lake Julia.

The swollen bases and the craggy tops of the cypresses are black silhouettes against the soft pale-orange illumination behind them.

Nothing is moving. It's as if we're looking at a still life painting in a quietly reverential art museum.

"Where are the kids?" I ask softly.

"Your dad and Verna took them to dinner and school clothes shopping."

"That's sweet."

"Went all the way out to Pier Park, so we have the evening to ourselves."

I squeeze her hand.

"You, sir, are going to get empty house sex."

I smile. "My favorite kind. Thank you."

"If you want it, of course. How are you?"

"I'm okay at the moment," I say. "Everything is tucked into its little box, and the lids are securely fastened."

"Good. How's the investigation going? Feel like talkin' about it?"

I share with her some of what I've learned recently.

"So Meg Stevens admits to having an altercation with Carla?"

"That's not how she characterizes it, but yeah."

"And her husband was sleeping with both victims—Carla and Olivia."

"Yeah, and one of Carla's friends to get back at her."

"For what exactly?"

I shrug. "Breaking it off, not letting him control her every move, just because . . . He wanted to punish and hurt her."

"Whatta guy," she says. "Sadist who uses sex as a weapon . . . and a wife who's attacking his conquests. Sounds like they need to move to the top of your suspect list."

I nod. "Already there. I'm going to re-interview both of them, get them on record, and see what the VSA says about what they claim, develop a timeline of their movements, build a case."

"You know . . ." Anna says, her eyes widening as an idea occurs to her. "It's possible that Meg is Olivia's stalker."

"Would explain why there has been so much threat of rape but no rape," I say.

"Yes, it would."

"What do you think's goin' on with Darlene?" she asks.

"Whatever it is, it ain't good. Looks like she's moved in, like she's taking advantage of a vulnerable victim. I'm gonna have to talk to Fred Miller about it."

"And she's gonna think it's because of the conflict y'all've had in the past."

I nod and frown. "She'll take it personally, and it will deteriorate our relationship even further. I made such a big mistake with her."

"You felt sorry for her."

"Not the first time that's gotten me into trouble," I say.

"Fine line between empathy and pity."

"One I fail to see most of the time."

We fall silent, and our attention returns to the lake.

The sky is a deeper orange now, the trees completely black, only a smudge of light remains low on the horizon, above it dark-blue twilight fading to night.

"Anything else helpful in her diary?"

"Not really. She didn't write in it a lot, and most of it is about John Paul and her desire to be a better mother for him. But I'm not finished with it yet."

"Figured out how you're going to prove paternity?" she asks.

"I'm going to politely ask them for their DNA," I say.

"And if they refuse?"

"I'm going to take it from the cup they drink from in the interview room or the envelop I ask them to seal once they sign the refusal and stick it inside."

CHAPTER
SIXTY-THREE

THAT NIGHT I have vivid dreams.

Waking often, I am unable to shake them, and they return the moment I'm back asleep.

Carla is hanging from the rope light in our foyer, the jumper cables dangling around her.

And though her neck is twisted and hanging limply to the side, she is alive and talking to me.

I am standing beneath her, my neck craned up and around to see her.

"It's my fault," she says.

"What is?"

"Me being dead."

I shake my head. "No, it's not."

"I don't mean that I caused it or anything, just that if I hadn't been doing what I was doing it wouldn't've happened."

"What do you mean? What were you doing?"

Her eyes are bloodshot with petechia hemorrhage from being strangled and her voice sounds hoarse from the fracture of her hyoid bone.

"Just that certain choices lead to others," she says. "Certain decisions put you more at risk than others. This wouldn't've happened if I had been at home with John Paul."

"That doesn't make it your fault or even make you remotely responsible."

"Simple victimology," she says. "Some people are far more at risk of becoming victims than others. Reggie's job put her at risk. My lifestyle puts me at risk."

I shake my head. "You are not responsible, but I'm going to catch whoever is."

"No, you're not," she says. "Not this time. And it's okay. It's not your fault. There's just not enough evidence. You'll be able to narrow it down to a few suspects, but you'll never know for sure who did it. Doesn't matter. No such thing as justice anyway. You know that."

I start to say something, but she is gone.

I'm in my truck, bouncing down a remote dirt road, Mason and Easton bound and gagged in the backseat.

Suddenly, we are in a clearing in the woods, and I have a shotgun pointed at them.

I can't figure out for sure which one killed Carla, so I've decided to kill them both.

Their frightened eyes are pleading.

Each of them is moaning and groaning frantically beneath their gag.

"Only one of you killed Carla, but neither of you is innocent. You treated her and every other woman in your life like property to use and abuse and disrespect and discard. But not anymore."

I jack a round into the chamber.

I shoot Mason full-blast, pointblank in the face. He's dead instantly, and half of his head is gone.

Easton collapses to the ground, screaming into his gag.

I do the same to him, only to the back of his head.

CHAPTER
SIXTY-FOUR

"I'VE ALREADY TOLD YOU," Mason Hayes is saying.

"Tell me again," I say.

We are in the interview room, and I've just asked him to take me through his movements last Sunday, the day Carla was killed.

I've already gone through the ten yes or no control questions for the VSA.

"Mason," I say, "this is a murder investigation. You are a suspect. You need to answer every question and do so honestly."

"I slept in," he says with a shrug. "I played some Grand Theft Auto. My mom brought me over some breakfast."

"What time was that?"

He shrugs. "No idea. Things are a little more laid back and relaxed when Dad is away, so—I'm sure Mom could tell you. Or it'll be on the security camera footage. Y'all have all that, don't you?"

"Then what?"

Another shrug.

In an attempt to act relaxed and disinterested, he comes across as dull and sleepy.

"I'd been texting Lily," he says. "I knew Joel was gonna be

out of town playing golf that day, so I hit her up. We started texting and . . . I asked her if she wanted to meet up and talk, go for a ride or somethin.' She said yeah, so we did. We rode around in my truck for a little while. Then we went for a boat ride. Took her on the river. Went to our camp and . . . you know. Then I took her back to her car."

"What did y'all do at the camp?" I ask. "How long were you there?"

"Fucked, okay. We fucked. We weren't there too long. She . . . she felt . . . bad, guilty like afterwards and wanted to go, so I took her back."

"Did you hurt her or do something to upset her?"

"*No*. No way. Absolutely not. She just felt bad about Joel. That was it. She's . . ."

"Got a conscience?" I offer.

He doesn't respond.

"How long have you been seeing her? How often do y'all—"

"That was the first and only time," he says. "I mean since we broke up way back when."

"Then what'd you do?"

"Grabbed a burger. Went home. Played some more Grand Theft. Took a nap. Later on . . . texted Carla. Asked her if she wanted to meet up, go for a ride. She said she did, and we did. We met at the end of the road. Rode around a little. She seemed . . . a little upset. Nothing big. Just a little sad. Seemed like she wanted to get back together or something. Took her back to her car. She followed me down to Tupelo Creek. We got in the boat and went down river. We . . . ah, made love. And when I started to leave, she refused. Said she wanted to stay longer and talk. But I was ready to go. I told her to come on, but she said no. I told her if she didn't come I was gonna leave her ass there. She said she wouldn't. So I left her. I wish I hadn't. But I had no way of knowing something would happen to her. I got in my boat and left. And I swear to almighty God that she was fine when I left. I went home. Ate. Played some Grand Theft. Passed out."

"You didn't go back to the camp?"

"No, sir, I did not."

"You didn't do anything with her car?"

He shakes his head. "No, sir, I did not. Well, I . . . She had left a hat and some sunglasses in my boat. I left them on her car, but that's all I did."

"What did y'all really fight about?" I ask.

"We didn't fight."

"How physical did it get?"

"It didn't."

"Did you hit her?"

"No, sir, I did not."

"Did you choke her?"

"No, sir, I did not."

"How about during sex?"

"No. It was just straight ol' sex. Nothing . . . too . . . It was just plain."

"What did y'all argue about?"

"I told you. She didn't want to go, and I was ready to go."

"I thought your plan was to take her to the landing and go back to the camp."

"It was."

"So you didn't want to go."

"I's ready to be by myself."

"Did she know you had been with Lily earlier?"

"No. Not . . . Lily. But she suspected I had been with somebody."

"At the cabin?"

"Yeah."

"Did you suspect her of being with somebody earlier also?"

"No."

"Did she tell you she had?"

"No. She . . . She wasn't like that."

"Like what?"

"You know how most people get real mean in an argument, try to say things to hurt you? She wasn't like that."

"Did she tell you she was pregnant?"

His eyes grow wide as surprise fills his face. "Was she?"

"Did she tell you?"

"No, sir, she did not."

"Did you believe her? Did you think it was yours?"

"She didn't tell me. I swear. Was she? Was it mine?"

"We need to do a DNA swab to find out," I say.

"No wonder she was acting so . . ."

"So what?"

"I don't know. Needy. Hormonal or whatever."

I open the file folder on the table beside me and pull out the swab.

"Are you willing to give us your DNA for a paternity test?"

He nods. "Yeah, but . . . who else you testin'?"

CHAPTER
SIXTY-FIVE

LATER THAT AFTERNOON I'm back in the same interview room. This time with Easton Stevens.

He's leaning back and slumped down in his chair, attempting to appear bored and unconcerned.

I've already gone through the ten yes or no control questions for the VSA.

"Hey," he says, "what happened to protecting my privacy?"

"This is a murder investigation," I say. "Besides, your wife already knows."

His eyes widen and he sits up a little. "Knows what? How do you know?"

"She knows about you," I say.

"What about me?"

"Your character. Your activities. She knew about you and Carla."

"Bullshit she did."

"She actually confronted her at the landing on Sunday."

"Bullshit she did."

"She did. We have a witness and Meg confirmed it."

"Fuck me."

"She didn't mention any of this to you?" I ask.

"No. All she talks about is the baby and what kind of family we're gonna be."

"Give me a detailed account of your movements last Sunday."

He sits back and assumes his previous nonchalant position. "Woke up."

"What time?"

"Nine-something. Not sure exactly."

"Meg was already out of bed. I was . . . We usually always have sex on Sunday morning when we wake up. I was bothered she was already up. Found her getting ready for church."

"Does she usually go to church on Sunday mornings?"

"Not really. Well, she didn't used to. She has more since she found out she was pregnant. Told me she'd expect me to go once the baby got here."

"Then what?"

"She was . . . acting . . . She was a little cold . . . distant. I guess I know why now. I got back in bed and started texting Carla. When Meg left . . . I went to meet her. We met at Iola Landing. She got in with me and we rode around. Little later on . . . we found a private spot in Iola and parked and talked and . . ."

"And?"

"Did . . . We had sex."

"Then what?"

"Talked some more. Then I took her back to the landing and left."

"When did you see her again?"

He shakes his head. "I didn't. That was the last time I ever saw her. I swear it."

"What'd you do then?"

"Went home. Wanted to be there before Meg got back."

"And were you?" I ask.

"Yeah. She . . ."

"She what?"

"She was late getting back from church," he says.

"That's because it wasn't church she was getting back from."

He shrugs.

"Do you think she lied to you about church and followed you and Carla?"

"No. No way. She wouldn't. And if she did . . . she wouldn't just watch while we fucked in my truck. She'd've . . ."

"Did you kill Carla?"

"No."

"Did Meg?"

"Absolutely not. Not in a millions years."

"Take me through the rest of your day."

"I cooked lunch. Did some chores around the house. Watched some TV. Nothing much really."

"What did Meg do?"

"Same stuff. Then went for a run and went grocery shopping."

"What did you do while she did that?"

"Just hung out. I don't know. Same stuff. House stuff. TV."

"What time did she get back?"

He shrugs. "Not sure. Wasn't too late."

"Did you go out again that afternoon or evening?"

"No, I don't think—Oh, yeah, I went for a ride. I like to put on music and ride the backroads."

"Did you see Carla?"

"While I was riding? I didn't see anybody."

"What time did you get back to your house?"

He shrugs. "Not sure. Seven or eight."

"Did you stop and get gas or anything while you were out riding?"

He nods. "Yeah. I grabbed some gas and road snacks at the new convenience store."

"Did you see Carla?"

"No."

"Mason Hayes?"

"No."

"Was your wife home when you got back?"

"She got back a little after me. But she wasn't out killin' Carla. I can tell you that."

"Did Carla tell you she was pregnant?"

"What? *No*. Was she?"

His surprise seems genuine.

"She didn't tell you that y'all were having a baby?"

"No. And we weren't. Meg and I are having a baby, not me and Carla."

"You were having a baby with both of them," I say. "Congratulations."

"No. I wasn't. If Carla was pregnant, it wasn't mine."

"If you're right then a paternity test will prove it."

"I ain't takin' no paternity test. It's not mine."

"It's a simple swab and will help us clear you."

He shakes his head.

"Are you refusing?"

"I damn sure am."

I open the file folder on the table beside me. Placing the swab to the side, I withdraw a piece of paper and an envelop.

"Sign this form saying you refuse," I say.

He does.

"Seal the envelop and initial the back."

He does.

"Put Sheriff Miller on the front and sign your name on it."

He does.

As he starts to stand, I say, "Just a couple more questions."

He sits back down.

"Are you having an affair with your neighbor, Olivia Nelson?"

"No."

"Have you ever been involved with her?"

He shakes his head, but there's no conviction in it.

"We need a verbal response for the recording."

"No," he says.

"I'm gonna ask you again, and I want you to think about a couple of things before you answer. Your wife said you were having an affair with Olivia Nelson. And we have software we run the interview recordings through that lets us know if you're lying. Are you or were you having an affair with Olivia Nelson?"

"I am not," he says. "When she first moved in . . . we . . . fooled around a little. Wasn't much to it, and it didn't last long. I love my wife and . . . the Nelson woman . . . It wasn't just that she was too old for me, but she was too . . . sad or something. I couldn't . . . deal with her . . . bullshit."

"Have you been harassing her?"

"Absolutely not."

"Has your wife?"

"No. Of course not."

"You don't sound too confident."

"Well, I am. She would never do anything like that to anyone."

"She assaulted Carla at the landing."

"If she did . . . that must've been hormones or something."

CHAPTER
SIXTY-SIX

"I'VE ALREADY TOLD you the truth about everything," Lillian Mosely is saying.

I nod and give her an expression that says I believe her. "We just have to have an official statement and interview recorded."

"Somehow it has gotten out," she says. "Everyone knows. Including Joel."

"Did you tell him or someone else?" I ask.

She frowns. "Someone else. I know you told me to tell him, and I was going to. I was trying to work up my nerve and . . . someone beat me to it."

There's an essential sadness to her that there wasn't before, a paleness and tension on her sweet face, and the bruise-like semi-circles beneath her eyes tell the story of sleepless nights.

"You were right," she says. "It should've come from me. I was . . . weak . . . and betrayed him twice. I'm sure you don't believe me, but . . . it's the only thing like that I've ever done. Ever. I've never cheated before. Never even come close—and not just on Joel. On anybody I've ever been with. I picked a hell of a time to be so stupid. And all because I was feeling fat and ugly and lonely and—How could I have been so . . ."

"Vulnerable," I say. "You were vulnerable. We all make our

greatest mistakes when we're weak and vulnerable, when we look outside of ourselves for answers and validation instead of going within to deal with the actual root issue."

"Sounds like you have some experience with it too."

"Of course. We all have."

"I feel so ashamed and . . . like I don't have a friend in the world. I feel like everyone is judging and condemning me and thinks I could be a murderer too."

I feel bad for her, and I know how self-sabotaging shame and guilt can be.

"Could I offer you a bit of advice?"

"Please."

"Know how I said not to compound your first mistake with a second one of not telling your husband?"

"Yeah?"

"Don't compound your mistakes by getting stuck. Own what you did. Examine why you did it. Do your best to address what led you to do it. Ask for forgiveness. And then forgive yourself and move on, attempting to truly learn from it and to be a more mindful and honest person. Getting stuck in guilt and shame doesn't fix anything, just gives a perverse sense of self-punishment."

"Thank you."

We are quiet a moment then transition to the interview, including the control questions.

She tells me essentially everything she has before in essentially the same order.

When we are done and she's getting ready to leave, she says, "Joel moved out. He's staying at his mom's."

"I'm sorry to hear that."

"I deserve it. Can't be with someone you can't trust."

"Maybe in time you can build back trust, repair the rupture, heal."

"Maybe."

"If that's what you want—"

"It is," she says. "More than anything."

"Then be sure to let him know."

"I have. I will."

"Don't say you'll do anything and don't be willing to. Don't let this mistake be something you are punished with—by him or you."

CHAPTER
SIXTY-SEVEN

"THIS IS RIDICULOUS," Meg Stevens says. "I've already told you everything."

Lily is gone, and now I'm in the interview room with Meg.

"We have to have a recording and an official statement," I say. "It protects you."

"I'm sure it does. Y'all are all about protecting people."

"And serving," I say, dryly with just a hint of sarcasm in my voice.

"In addition to having your statement and interview on record," I say, "we have deception-detecting software that we run everything through."

"Oh," she says, sitting up and becoming more serious. "Like a lie detector without being hooked up to a machine?"

"Something like that."

"Well, it's a good thing I always tell the truth."

"Let's start with you taking me through your day last Sunday."

She does, including her confrontation with Carla.

"Your husband says you went for a run that evening,"

She nods. "I run every day."

"Did anyone see you?"

"I'm sure they did, but I can't remember anyone in particular."

"Well, give me your route and the time you started and stopped and we'll see if anyone can remember seeing you."

"He said you also went to the grocery store."

"Clearly he remembers this day far better than I do. If he says that's what I did, then I'm sure that's what I did."

"Remembering talking to anyone or—"

"I don't even remember going."

"Try to remember, and if you could find your receipt that would be helpful too."

"Is all this necessary?"

"Neither you or your husband have an alibi for the time that Carla was killed," I say.

"Yes, we do. He was home and I was running and apparently grocery shopping."

"Obviously, we can't corroborate him being home alone, but we'd at least like to be able rule you out if we can."

"I'll look for the damn receipt."

"And we'll pull the security camera footage from the store. Did you go to the IGA or—"

"Yeah. Now I remember. I only grabbed a few things to make dinner with that night, so I wasn't there long, but . . . I was gone for quite a while. I drove around thinking about everything. How immature and selfish Easton is. I was . . . I was considering terminating my pregnancy. I just wanted to think about things for a while."

"Where'd you go? Anyone see you? Did you talk to anyone? Use your phone?"

"No. I just drove around."

"Okay," I say. "We'll get your cell records to see if we can track your movements based on the pings on the towers."

"You can do that?" she asks, alarmed.

I nod.

"Well, all I did was ride around. Doesn't matter what the towers say."

"Have you ever harassed or gotten into a confrontation with Olivia Nelson?"

"What?" she asks, her voice rising, her face registering her surprise.

She is completely unprepared for the question.

"Ah, no. Of course not. Who says I have?"

"You assaulted Carla because she slept with your husband. You didn't do the same to Olivia Nelson?"

"I . . . I didn't assault Carla. I haven't assaulted anyone. I'm not a . . . I don't assault people."

"You're not harassing Olivia Nelson, paying her back for sleeping with your husband?"

"She's a sad, old loony tunie. I wouldn't—"

"Didn't Easton's mother die when he was young?"

"Yeah. Why? We didn't have anything to do with that."

"And wasn't he raised by a single father?"

"Yeah."

"So he probably has mother issues," I say. "Was or is Olivia Nelson a mother figure for him? Is that why she's such a threat?"

"She's not a threat at all. You're . . . You must be projecting your own mother issues onto him. Wasn't your mother a drunk and a—"

"That must be it," I say. "So we're not going to find your fingerprints and DNA in Olivia's house?"

"I didn't say I'd never been in there."

"What have you been in there for?"

"Visiting?"

"You visit with the woman your husband is having an affair with?"

"What does this have to do with Carla's death? Why are you asking me all these crazy questions? How dare you speak to me like this?"

CHAPTER
SIXTY-EIGHT

"I WANT you to take his gun and his badge right now," Hank Stevens is saying.

The three of us are in Fred Miller's office, where Hank, Easton's dad and a prominent business person and county commissioner, is calling for my job.

He's a fleshy, perpetually sunburned and liquored up older man with closely cropped gray hair and bloodshot icy blue eyes. Of average height and build, he's thick and meaty, and the face of his skin is pocked with acne scars. As if a uniform, he's wearing what he always seems to be wearing—pressed khakis, brown work boots, and a sky-blue Columbia fishing shirt.

"For what?" I ask. "Interviewing your son?"

Miller says, "Hank, settle down and tell me what your complaint is."

"He is destroying the lives and families of good people," he says. "People who matter in this community."

"You sayin' some people matter and others like Carla don't?" I ask.

"See?" he says. "He's unhinged. Trampling all over good people and making a mess of everything. It's some kind of personal vendetta. He was way too close to this thing. You should've never allowed him to work this case."

"Be careful, Hank," Miller says. "Don't tell me how to run my department or do my job."

"Somebody needs to. I know you're new, but . . . my God. We finally got rid of that crazy bitch who was in here before, and now you're actin' just like her."

I step over to Hank, my fists clinched at my sides. "I'd strongly recommend you show some respect to our former sheriff."

Miller says, "And I'd strongly suggest you show some respect to the current sheriff."

I stand there in Steven's face, hoping he will hit me or shove me or something, but he doesn't. Instead he takes a deep breath and a step back.

"Look," he says. "Neither of you want me for an enemy. I can assure you of that."

"We don't have to be enemies," Miller says. "Just tell me your complaint with respect and civility."

"I have," he says. "He is harassing my family. It's police brutality."

"*Police brutality*?" I say.

"Yeah."

I shake my head. "It's no wonder nothing means anything any more. For someone like you to use a phrase like that for lawful and respectful interviews is . . . absolutely absurd."

"You're trying to break up my son's marriage," he says. "You told his wife he was involved with the victim and that Nelson woman."

"Actually, she told me," I say.

He whips his head around at me, a surprised look on his face.

"And as far as the treatment of your family . . . Not only did I keep my initial conversation with your son quiet, I didn't arrest him for assaulting a law enforcement officer when he hit me in the back of the head with the butt of his rifle."

"That's . . . He didn't do that."

"Yes, he did," Miller says.

"Claims he didn't know it was me," I say. "It was at night in the wooded lot between his house and Olivia Nelson's. I can still arrest him for it."

His posture and demeanor changes. "All I'm sayin' is you can't just run roughshod over people, especially the family members of community leaders."

"I haven't," I say. "I've done just the opposite."

"Well . . . this case is too personal for you." He turns to Miller. "You know he shouldn't be working it."

"Which case is that?"

"You know damn well which case. Carla Pearson."

"That's Arnie Ward's case. John is working the Olivia Nelson case."

"And your son was involved with both victims," I say.

"He likes women and they like him. That's it. He's never hurt anyone. Would never harm or harass anyone."

"Then we'll clear him," I say. "But if you're wrong about him —like you've been wrong about everything else you've said in here today . . ."

CHAPTER
SIXTY-NINE

"HE'S GONNA BE A PROBLEM," Miller is saying.

Hank Stevens is gone, and the two of us are alone in his office with the door closed.

I nod.

"No special treatment for his family, but be careful and be sure about everything. His son still a suspect?"

I nod. "Son and daughter-in-law. And in both cases."

"No wonder he's coming on so strong," he says.

"Tread carefully."

"I have been and will continue to."

When Fred Miller first took over for Reggie, I wasn't sure I was going to be able to work for him. And though I'll never respect him as much or be as close to him as Reggie, working for him is far better than I ever thought it could be. He's more of a politician than a cop, but so far he's made the cop call when he's really needed to.

"He's not wrong, you know," Miller says. "You are too close. The case is too personal. No way you should be working it."

"I'm just helping Arnie out where I can."

"Don't kid a kidder," he says. "Thing is . . . you've shown great restraint so far and you're . . . handling yourself and the

whole situation well. That's why you're still on it. If that changes
. . . No matter how much I don't want to lose you . . . I won't
have any choice."

I nod. "I understand."

"Please don't make me regret this."

"I need to talk to you about something," I say.

"Okay," he says.

"Just want to bring this to your attention."

"Okay."

"From what I can tell, it looks like Darlene has all but moved
in with Olivia Nelson."

"Oh, really."

"I think Olivia Nelson is a very vulnerable person," I say.
"And I just want to make sure we're not taking advantage of that
or crossing any lines that might . . . be exploitative."

"Thanks for letting me know," he says. "I appreciate it. I'll
look into it. Keep an eye on it."

"We could rotate who watches her," I say. "I could pick up a
shift or two. So could Arnie. We could use some of the deputies.
But unlike Darlene, we'd all stay outside of the home in our
vehicles."

"That's a good idea."

Arnie taps on the door, and Miller waves him in.

"I've gone over the VSAs from the interviews."

I had asked Arnie to examine them because he's the best
and most qualified with the software and with reading the
results.

"Come on in," he says. "Grab Darlene too."

When we are all seated in his office, Miller says, "Figure this
would be a good time for us to go over everything we have, see
where we are with both cases. But before we get to that . . . I
want everyone to take a shift at Olivia Nelson's. It's not fair to
have Darlene take them all."

"I don't mind," Darlene says. "It's no problem. I'm the only
one without a family."

"John, you take tonight. Arnie you take tomorrow night. Then we'll get a rotation of deputies too."

Darlene glances at me for a moment and seems to be trying to work something out.

"Now, Arnie, what have we got?"

"Bottom line is this," Arnie says. "Mason Hayes and Lillian Mosely show very little deception, but Easton and Meg Stevens show quite a bit."

Just then Rudy, reeking of alcohol, slings the door open and steps inside.

"I wanna repor' a kidnappin'," he exclaims to Miller. He has a difficult time getting the words out. "This man . . ." He points a shaking finer at me. "Has stolen my gran' . . . son. And . . . fur . . . more . . . plans to conduct . . . illegal . . . funeral for my daughter without . . . me . . . father."

I stand. "Rudy, we haven't kidnapped your grandson. We're taking care of him. Just like we always have. You can see him anytime you like—when you're sober. And I asked you about the funeral. We talked about it. Don't you remember?"

He takes a swing at me.

I pull my head back, and he misses.

The momentum of his missed punch pitches him forward, and he falls to the ground.

"You . . . all . . . saw that," he says. "He . . . threw me to . . . ground. An old man. Sheriff . . . do your job and 'rrest him."

CHAPTER
SEVENTY

THAT EVENING before heading over to Olivia Nelson's place, I spend as much time with my family as possible, trying to connect with each one individually.

I've already listened to a new song Nash is working on, helped Johanna with her homework, played Pop the Pig and Greedy Granny with Taylor, and slow danced in the kitchen with Anna while helping her with dinner.

At the moment, I'm playing with John Paul in the living room.

We are on the floor playing with an elaborate track where jeeps try to escape dinosaurs. The set, which includes 144 track pieces, 4 palm trees, 2 dinosaurs, 2 dinosaur jeeps, 8 traffic signs, and 4 jeep tires, takes up most of the middle of the living room.

He's wearing a tiny red and white Wewa Gators jersey and gray athletic shorts and has the largest dinosaur in his right hand.

"Can't wait 'til I'm bigger and can be one of the teamers," he says.

"It won't be long," I say. "And you'll make a great teamer. How was your day at school today? Who'd you play with?"

He pushes one of the jeeps off the track with the head of his dinosaur.

"Jackson and Stephen," he says.

"What'd y'all play?"

"Pirates on the playground. But . . . Millie said I couldn't play 'cause I didn't have a mommy. But Jackson said I could too play, and you didn't have to have a mommy to play pirates. And Stephen said most pirates didn't have mommies."

"I'm so sorry Millie said that. That was not nice of her at all. How'd it make you feel when she said that?"

"Sad. Made me miss mommy."

"Does Miss Rylee know she said it?"

"Yeah. She made her stand on the wall for the rest of playtime."

He replaces the jeep back on the track and has his dinosaur roar at it.

"I'm so sorry she said that, buddy," I say and give him a hug.

He hugs me back, pressing his dinosaur into the side of my face.

"How do you feel now?"

"Okay," he says with a little shrug.

"Do you have any idea how much I love you?" I ask.

He nods.

"So, so much," I say. "I'll always love you and take care of you and—"

"Will you be my daddy?" he asks, his soft, sweet little voice slaying me.

"Absolutely," I say. "I would love to be. I'd be so honored."

"Can I live with you and Anna and Taylor and Johanna and Nash always?"

"Always and forever."

"Good. I want to. And I want you to be my daddy. I want Anna to be my family, but . . . I already have a mommy. She's up in heaven now."

"We will be whatever you want us to be. And we'll always be your family. And we'll always take good care of you."

CHAPTER
SEVENTY-ONE

"I'M gonna be out here all night," I say to Olivia Nelson.

I am standing on her stoop, while she's in her partially open doorway.

"I'll keep an eye on the place. I want you to feel safe. Here's my cell number." I hand her a business card with my number written on the back, even though it's printed on the front as well. "Call me if you need anything. I'll be right out here."

"Where is Susan?" she asks.

"Who?" I ask.

"Ah, Darlene," she says. "She prefers her middle name. Where is she tonight?"

"We're all taking turns," I say. "She has the night off."

She gives a little frown and a quick nod. "I'll miss her."

"You two seem close," I say.

"She's been so great. Never felt safer in my entire life."

"Everyone in our agency is working hard to keep you safe and find out who's harassing you."

"I know and appreciate it. It's just . . . so lonely out here. Susan was the first person I've really connected with since I've been here. I'm not good at making new friends, let alone lovers."

"Are you and Darlene having an intimate relationship?"

She gives me a coy little smile. "I'm not one to kiss and tell."

"Have you received any other communications from your stalker?" I ask.

She shakes her head. "I think he knows Susan has been here."

I nod. "That's probably it."

"Will you come in?" she says. "I'm making dinner."

"I'll be right out here in my vehicle. Call me if you need anything."

"What I *need*—or at least could use—is some company."

"I understand," I say. "I'm sorry I can't provide that. I'm on duty and have to concentrate on keeping you safe."

She shakes her head, her face conveying what a disappointment I am, steps back, and closes the door.

I go back to my car and begin to return calls I haven't gotten to today.

I call Michelle first.

"Sorry it's taken me so long to get back with you," I say.

"No worries. Just wanted to give you an autopsy update. ME's not gonna release the final autopsy or give an official cause of death until he gets toxicology back—and that's gonna be a few weeks . . . but he wants us to know he's leaning toward homicide. He believes a ligature was used, which is what makes it easier to hide with the hanging, but he's seeing petechiae in the eyes and ears, some blood congestion in the face, and signs of both the inverted V of hanging where the rope rode up her neck, and he's seeing the level rope marks consistent with ligature strangulation. They're subtle, but they're there. He thinks the strangulation happened quickly and the staged hanging took place very soon after."

"He's just confirming what we already know," I say.

"But it's good to have it," she says. "And we'll need the autopsy to rule her death a homicide to make a case and get a conviction."

"True," I say. "What about—"

I stop as I see Darlene pull into Olivia's driveway and get out in casual clothes and walk toward the side door.

"Let me call you back," I say and end the call.

Jumping out of my truck, I rush over to Darlene.

"What're you doin'?" I ask.

"Whatever the hell I please," she says. "I'm off duty. It's none of your business, but I'm having dinner with Liv."

"You need to leave," I say. "Doesn't matter that you're off duty."

"Never figured you for a homophobe," she says.

"I'm not and you know it. You can't be involved with a victim."

"And you can't investigate your daughter's death," she says.

"Carla wasn't my daughter."

"Might as well have been, and you know good and goddamn well you shouldn't be investigating it, but you are. I'm tired of you being the only one who can do whatever the fuck you want to do."

With that, she turns and walks to the door where Olivia is waiting for her.

CHAPTER
SEVENTY-TWO

I'M THINKING about and preparing my eulogy for Carla's funeral when the call comes.

It's later that night.

I'm in my truck, the interior light on, jotting down ideas in my notebook.

"John," Olivia says, her voice faint, barely above a whisper. "John . . . I've . . . been . . . attacked. Help me."

I'm out of the truck and running toward the house.

"Where are you?" I ask.

She doesn't respond.

Though I've been watching them and know no one has entered or exited from the front or side doors, I check both.

They are locked.

"Where are you?" I ask again.

And again get no response.

I sprint around the side of the house to the back.

As I run, I scan the backyard for movement.

I've been walking the perimeter every half-hour, so it hasn't been long since I've been back here.

I haven't seen or heard anything suspicious tonight, and with my truck in the front yard and Darlene's car alongside

Olivia's in the driveway, I really didn't expect him to try anything.

In the back, I find the newly repaired sliding glass door open slightly.

Withdrawing my weapon, I enter the house.

Everything is quiet, and I can detect no movement.

The only light in the kitchen and living room comes from the hood of the stove, but it's enough to see.

In the dimness I can see that the rooms are empty and there are no signs of violence.

Continuing down the short hallway, I find the door to Olivia's bedroom slightly ajar.

I enter to find Darlene asleep face down on the left side of the bed and the covers on Olivia's side pulled back.

I quickly scan the room then check the bathroom.

"Darlene," I say. "Darlene."

She doesn't rouse.

I shake her with one hand and call her name more loudly.

She still doesn't move.

I feel for a pulse.

She's alive. I push her over and quickly examine her.

There are no signs of trauma, but she is out and nothing I do rouses her.

I quickly check the other two bedrooms and their Jack and Jill bathroom, then the formal living room, laundry room, and garage.

Olivia is not in the house, and there are no signs of a struggle anywhere.

I run out of the house and into the backyard.

Pausing for a moment, I scan the area again, attempting to keep my eyes wide and unfocused, alert for figures or movement in the darkness.

Then I see it.

In the far back corner, near the tree line of the wooded lot, I can see the faint glow of Olivia's phone.

I race toward it.

Crossing the yard as quickly as I can, running around the old playhouse and storage shed, and weaving in and out of the scattered pines, I arrive at the phone to find it still in Olivia's outstretched hand.

I drop to the ground beside her.

She appears unconscious but alive.

Her face is bruised, her nose bleeding, and a ligature is tied tightly around her neck.

I call for an ambulance and backup as I untie the ligature and try to get her to wake up.

She screams as she becomes conscious and tries to fight me off.

"It's John. You're okay. You're safe now."

"John?"

"Yes. You're safe."

"Oh, John, thank God."

"Who attacked you?" I ask. "What happened?"

She shakes her head. "I don't know. I don't . . . I can't . . . remember anything."

She attempts to sit up, and I help her.

"Why can't I remember?" she says. "What is . . ."

"What's the last thing you remember?"

"Having dinner with Susan . . . Having some wine . . . Going to bed . . . That's it. I . . . I'm not gonna survive this, am I?"

CHAPTER
SEVENTY-THREE

"I WAS DRUGGED," Darlene is saying.

It's the next morning.

Arnie, Darlene, Michelle, and I are with the sheriff in his office.

I nod. "I believe you were."

Michelle says, "We're testing the wine and the leftover food, but it will take a while."

"Did you have anything to drink or eat that Olivia didn't?" I ask.

She shrugs. "I don't think so."

Olivia is still at Sacred Heart, where she was taken last night. I asked Za to examine her and to have the psychiatrist on call do the same.

Miller looks at me. "How did he get in and get her out of the house without you seeing?"

"He didn't," I say.

Everyone turns and looks at me.

"I kept a close eye on the house and walked around the yard often. I had a visual on the front and side door at all times. The only door I didn't have eyes on the entire time was the back sliding glass door. It's new. Only Olivia has a key. It wasn't forced or broken into. All the windows and doors were locked. No one broke into that house. No one attacked Olivia. She's doing it to herself."

"What?" Miller says.

Darlene shakes her head and says, "No fuckin' way."

"She drugged you. She's the only one who could. She inflicted the wounds onto herself, crept out of the house and laid in the backyard until I got there."

"You've lost your fuckin' mind," Darlene says. "Must be how fucked up you are from Carla's death. And I get it, but damn."

"With all her alleged attacks," I say, "we don't have a single shred of evidence that someone did any of it to her. None. No prints. No DNA. And for everything we only have her word for it."

Darlene looks at the others. "Tell me y'all aren't buyin' this bullshit."

"I'm listening," Miller says. "Haven't bought anything yet."

"I'm inclined to agree with John," Arnie says. "It's the only thing that fits all the evidence."

"There's no escalation," I say. "He threatens her. Says he's going to rape and kill her. He has ample opportunities but never does it—just does the same thing over and over. And all while we are watching her, guarding her—and with one of our investigators in the bed with her. It just doesn't fit."

"Roy has you so fuckin' fooled," Darlene says.

"If he does," I say, "or if it's someone else—like Easton or Meg Stevens—then we're dealing with the perfect criminal mastermind who is invisible and leaves no clues."

"Roy is a genius," she says. "He is. He knows what he's doin'."

"I asked both a medical doctor and a psychiatrist to examine her," I say. "They both agree with me. The psychiatrist says she wants to do far more tests and exams to be able to say for sure and to even begin to give a diagnosis, but from her preliminary exam . . . she concluded that Olivia is deeply disturbed. I'd like to interview her and see what the VSA says about her level of deception, because I'm not convinced she even knows she's doing it. And I'd like to ask her to submit to a thorough psych eval."

"I'll be damned," Miller says. "If you're right . . . Never seen anything like this."

"He's not right," Darlene says. "For fuck sake, don't listen to this deranged bullshit. He's the one who's sick."

"You have no objectivity or credibility," Miller says. "You're sleepin' with the victim."

"I'm close enough to her and the situation to see what's going on."

"I have no choice but to place you on suspension," he says.

"He's the one who needs to be suspended," she says, jerking her head toward me. "Not me. You're letting him work Carla's case, but you're sending me home. This is such bullshit. Is it because I'm a woman or a lesbian? You know I'm the only one who supported your campaign. This is how you repay me? Well, let me ask you this. When Roy kills Olivia, will you even suspend John then? All y'all are doing by drinkin' the fuckin' John Jordan Kool-Aid is signing that poor woman's death warrant."

CHAPTER
SEVENTY-FOUR

WHEN I GET HOME that evening, a social worker from the Florida Department of Children and Families is there.

Her name is Cassandra King, and both Anna and I have worked with her over the years and count her as a friend.

She is a largish middle-aged African-American woman with glasses and lots and lot of thick, curly black hair.

"Y'all know why I'm here," she says. "Rudy Pearson is petitioning for custody of John Paul. And he keeps calling the abuse hotline and accusing y'all of abuse."

"Oh my God," Anna says.

"I know," Cassandra says. "I know John Paul is where he's supposed to be, but . . ."

"We want to adopt him," Anna says.

She nods. "Okay. We can certainly get to that, but for now we've got to deal with Rudy."

"This is where John Paul wants to be," Anna says.

"Where he needs to be," I say. "Where Carla would want him to be."

"I don't doubt that, but it'd be so much easier if she'd left a will saying that."

"What can we do so this has the least impact on John Paul?" I ask. "He's been through so much. We don't want his life disrupted any more than it already has."

"I'll do an interview with him today and recommend he stay with y'all for now, but we need to get affidavits from any of Carla's friends who may have heard her say or imply she'd want him with you two. And continue going through her paperwork and make sure she didn't put it in writing somewhere."

"I'll have another look through her papers," I say.

"Here's my concern," she says. "Rudy's not going to get custody, but we don't want him to continue to raise such a stink that DCF is forced to place John Paul in a group or foster home."

"Oh my God," Anna says. "That could happen?"

I shake my head. "We can't let that happen. No matter what."

"That would be so traumatizing to him," Anna says. "To us all. He's already lost his mother. He can't lose the only other family he has."

CHAPTER
SEVENTY-FIVE

"I'M GOING to drive over to Pottersville and speak with Rudy," I say.

It's later that night. We've just finished cleaning up after dinner. Taylor and John Paul are playing in the living room, Johanna is doing homework at the kitchen table, and Nash is playing guitar in his room.

"I'm not sure that's such a good idea," she says. "We don't want to make things worse."

"How could they get worse?"

She shrugs. "I don't know exactly, but I feel like they could. Maybe I should talk to him."

"Maybe we both should," I say. "Maybe we should take John Paul with us so he can visit with him and see we're not trying to keep him from him."

"Maybe," she says.

"Or maybe we should do it tomorrow," I say. "Earlier in the day. He's probably passed out by now."

She lowers her voice. "We can't let . . . anyone take him. Can you imagine that poor little fella in a group home?"

"We're not gonna let that happen," I say. "We'll—"

I stop as I see headlights in our driveway.

"Who is it?" she asks.

"Not sure. I'll go check."

I step over to the side door and open it.

Olivia Nelson is getting out of her car.

I close the door behind me and walk out to meet her.

"Hey," she says. "Sorry to barge in on you like this."

Her voice is hoarse and low.

"How are you feeling?" I ask.

"I'm okay," she says. "Listen . . . I just want to say . . . I understand you think I'm making all this up . . . for . . . attention or something. But I'm not. I swear to you I'm not. I could never do . . ." She touches her throat. ". . .something like this to myself."

"Did Darlene tell you?" I ask.

"Yeah. She's just worried about me and doesn't want . . . She says everybody listens to you. She's concerned that because of what you're sayin' everyone will stop searching for my stalker and stop protecting me and that something really bad will happen. I don't want to die."

"We're continuing to investigate," I say. "And we'll still be providing security. I believe Arnie Ward is at your house waiting for you right now. But you can help us by submitting to the exam and taking the tests."

"I will," she says. "'Cause I'm not makin' this up. I'm not doing this to myself. I couldn't. Please believe me. Please don't let him win, don't let him kill me."

"Who?" I ask.

"I honestly don't know," she says, her voice quavering. "I'd tell you if I did. Sometimes I think it's Roy. Others, Easton. But sometimes . . . I think it's a woman. Is that possible? Could a woman be doing this to me? But that is what you believe, isn't it? You think a woman is doing this to me. You just think it's me."

CHAPTER
SEVENTY-SIX

AT A LITTLE AFTER ten that night, I meet Jordan Grant and Bailey Bozeman at Lake Alice Park.

Jordan just ended her shift at the Dollar Store across the street and walked over.

"Thank y'all for meetin' me," I say. "I know it's late. I won't take too much of your time."

I apologize to them even though they set the time and the place of our meeting. I'm sure Jordan is tired from working and ready to get home to her boys.

"I only have a few minutes," Bailey says. "Have somewhere I have to be."

I nod.

"Two quick things," I say. "I'm working on Carla's funeral and wanted to see if either of you would like to say or read anything at it or if you know of anyone who would."

They both sort of frown and shake their heads.

"I know I have a big mouth and talk all the damn time," Bailey says, "but I can't stand up in front of people and . . . especially at something like that."

"I can't," Jordan says.

Even in the dim light of the park, her toffee skin glows and her huge black eyes sparkle. But as beautiful as she is, she could be even more so if it weren't for . . . something in her countenance. I can't tell if it's fatigue or an essential sadness, but something is weighing her down.

"Do either of you know anyone who would?" I ask. "I don't want to leave anyone out."

They shrug and shake their heads.

"Nobody comes to mind," Bailey says.

"Okay, well, let me know if you think of anyone. I'm working on her eulogy. Let me know anything you think should be included. Please share with me any memories or stories about her that you have. You both have my number."

"Most of my stories you can't say in church," Bailey says.

"The second thing I wanted to talk to you two about is John Paul," I say. "Anna and I love him like a son and want to adopt him."

"Y'all should," Bailey says. "Y'all've already been helpin' raise him."

"Rudy is fighting us for custody and—"

"That drunk bastard can't raise himself," Bailey says. "Hell, he didn't raise Carla. Damn sure ain't gonna raise her son. Probably just wants free labor for his shitty restaurant."

"Did Carla ever say anything to either of you about who she wanted to take care of John Paul if anything ever happened to her?"

"I just always assumed it'd be y'all," Bailey says.

Jordan says, "A long time ago she asked me to help y'all and to stay in his life if anything happened to her."

"Would y'all be willing to give a statement to DCF about Carla's wish for John Paul?"

They nod.

"I gotta dip," Bailey says. "Just let me know what I can do and when. Can't let that wino get his hands on that cute little fella."

"Thanks," I say. "I'll be in touch."

When Bailey pulls away, I say to Jordan, "I'll walk you over to your car."

We begin to head in that direction, crossing the street in front of the park, then the grass of the small lot, and pausing at the sidewalk next to Main Street.

"You okay?" I ask.

She nods. "Yeah."

"Is anything wrong?"

She shakes her head. "Just feel bad for Carla—and for John Paul."

"Did Carla say anything about us taking in John Paul more recently?"

She shrugs. "Not to me. But we haven't hung out as much lately."

As we cross Main Street, there are no vehicles visible in either direction, just the empty road illuminated by street lamps and business signs.

"Is that because you slept with Easton?" I ask.

Tears fill her eyes and begin to stream down her cheeks.

She nods as she wipes them. "I feel so . . . ashamed and . . . guilty. I . . . I shouldn't have done it, but . . . they had both told me it was over between them and had been for a while. I still shouldn't have done it. He's married. But he caught me at a very low time. I just . . . I'm so lonely most of the time. All I do is take care of my boys and work. That's it. And . . . Anyway . . . the only reason he did it was to hurt her. He told her as soon as we had done it. Even took a picture of us without me knowing it and sent it to her. It really hurt her. Which I get. I was so, so, so, so stupid. She didn't really get mad at me, just hurt. She didn't . . . . All she did was let me know she knew and then just sort of cut me off. We had never been close, but she was a friend—one of the few I had. Anyway . . . She wanted y'all to have John Paul. I'd be happy to give a statement to DCF. But I don't think she'd even want me at her funeral—let alone sayin' something."

CHAPTER
SEVENTY-SEVEN

WHEN I GET HOME, Merrill is waiting for me in the driveway.

He's leaning against his car, a Black Sapphire Metallic 3 Series BMW.

I park, turn off my truck, walk over, and join him.

"How are you?" he asks.

I shrug. "'Bout how you'd expect."

He nods. "Figured. What can I do?"

"Can't think of anything at the moment."

"Got a little gift for you," he says. "Santa Merrill comin' early this year. Coulda just called you and told you, but I wanted to see how you were doing."

"You see it," I say.

He shakes his head. "Be hard enough if it was just one of 'em, but . . . losing Reggie and Carla . . . and so close together . . . that's a wicked combination punch. Not surprised you still standin', but . . . you look a little wobbly."

I nod. "I am."

"Hear Rudy wants to take JP away from y'all?"

"You got good sources."

"Well, you can mark that one off your list of shit to worry about."

"Oh, yeah?"

"Ol' Rudy ain't gonna be a problem any more—at least not relating to JP's custody."

"Is that the present in Santa Merrill's sleigh?"

He nods. "I've been watching his ass more closely since I heard he been harassin' y'all."

Merrill is an investigator with the sheriff's office in Potter County where Rudy lives.

"Figured shit was hard enough right now without him tryin' to take JP off your hands. Now, I know his ass is drunk most of the time, but I know he's the most fucked up at night. So I've just been waiting for him to venture out at night. And sure enough . . . low and behold tonight he went out—probably 'cause he ran out of booze. And guess what he got . . . That's right. Another DUI, but not only another DUI. He's still not supposed to be driving from his last one, so he upsized his shit with driving with a suspended license, driving without insurance and . . . best of all . . . assault on a law enforcement officer. He's in our jail even as we speak, so . . . not that anybody with a lick of sense was gonna give JP to him anyway, but now there's no way the dimmest DCF worker in the state would. Ho ho ho. Merrilly Christmas, motherfuckers."

CHAPTER
SEVENTY-EIGHT

THE NEXT MORNING when I enter Rudy's cell in the Potter County Jail, he's sitting on his bunk, his head hanging down.

He looks up at me, his bloodshot eyes filled with sadness and shame.

"You here to gloat?" he asks.

"I'm here to drive you home," I say. "And I brought your grandson."

His eyes widen, and he tilts his head forward. "Why?"

"We will never keep him from you," I say. "You'll always be his grandfather and will always be in his life."

"I will?"

"Of course."

What I don't tell him is that we'll never leave John Paul alone with him or take him around him when he's drunk.

I've seen cases where having a grandchild is the thing that finally gets some addicts clean and sober, but it's rare. For both Rudy and John Paul's sake, I hope that happens here.

"We've never kept John Paul away from you and never will," I say. "We'll take excellent care of him and raise him as our own. Carla wanted us to have him because she knew how much we love him and how good his life would be with us. Her friends are going to testify to that. We're going to get him. You can keep fighting us on it, or you can spend that time working on being the best grandpa you can be to your grandson."

"You . . . didn't have to come today," he says. "Any hope I had of getting him is . . . gone. I appreciate what you're doing and that you brought John Paul to see me. I won't fight y'all anymore. Just don't take him away from me."

"We won't."

"He's all I've got left."

"Then live like it," I say. "Find a meeting. Get sober. Set a good example for your grandson."

"I know you won't believe me, but I'm going to," he says. "I am."

"Prove me and everyone else wrong. Get clean and sober. Put your life back together. I'll drive you to a meeting anytime day or night."

"I'm gonna do it," he says.

I hold little hope that he actually will, but I'm pulling for him to and will do anything I can to help him do it.

"I want to say something at Carla's funeral," he says.

"Good," I say.

"And I want her buried in our family plot in Pottersville."

"Of course."

Tears fill his eyes. "I can't believe she's really gone."

"Me either."

"Thank you," he says.

I don't know what he's thanking me for, but I give him a small nod.

"For . . . everything," he says. "For coming here this morning like this. For bringing John Paul. And . . . for all you did for Carla for . . . while she was alive. All you're still doin' for her."

Blinking back tears of my own, I say, "Let's get you cleaned up and out of here so you can go see your grandson."

CHAPTER
SEVENTY-NINE

CARLA'S FUNERAL is a very sad affair—and not only in the way that most funerals are sad.

There is plenty of grief, the soul crushing sadness of loss, especially the loss of someone so young, of a mother who leaves behind a small child, but there is something else.

It's how poorly attended and sort of pitiful the whole thing is.

Is this all her life comes down to? A few random mourners—most of whom have more of a connection to me and Anna than Carla.

We are beneath a funeral home open air tent next to her coffin, which is suspended above her open grave. Five short rows of bent and warped unpadded metal folding chairs on the fake green turf of indoor/outdoor carpet, and there are too many empty chairs.

It's stiflingly hot even in the shake beneath the tent, and no breeze stirs the thick, humid air.

In many ways Carla's life is over before it really began, and that sense of tragic waste permeates the atmosphere.

I always attempt to make the memorials and funerals I do celebrations of the person's life, an honoring of their time and talents and the way they touched the people who knew them, and though this funeral is no exception it's more difficult because of the brevity and insular nature of her existence.

I reflect on our time together over the years, the memories of her strength and independence. I concentrate on her love for and adoration of John Paul.

John Paul sits on Anna's lap in the front row with the rest of our children and Rudy, who is somber and attentive.

I think about the fact that his mother was herself motherless, but because of her and because of Anna he never will be.

Among the few people in attendance are my dad and Verna, Merrill and Za, Fred Miller, Arnie, Michelle Quinn, Bailey Bozeman, and Jordan Grant.

A few of Rudy's diner's regulars are present. As is John Paul's teacher.

Mason Hayes is in attendance with his parents.

Not surprisingly, Easton, Meg, and Hank are not present.

"I wanted so much more for her," I am saying.

My mouth is dry and my throat hoarse.

"Much more of this life and the possibilities each new day brings. I wanted her to get to watch her sweet boy grow into a good man. I wanted her to find what she was meant to do—in addition to being John Paul's mom—and be able to experience the joy of doing it. I wanted to get to watch her find her way and grow into a wise, mature woman. I wanted so much more for her. And I certainly didn't want her life to end the way it did. But I don't get what I want. So I grieve today. I stand before you and share my sadness. I share my joy too—the joy of knowing Carla and having so many great memories, so many meaningful times. I just wanted more—and not just for me and for you, but mostly for her."

Following the funeral, several of those in attendance tell me what a good job I did honoring her and expressing our collective grief, but I'm numb and don't feel I did justice to Carla, her short life, her tragic death.

CHAPTER
EIGHTY

I'M SO overwhelmed with sadness as I drive home from Carla's funeral, so frustrated at not being able to help her that I have the strong urge to do something for someone, to reach out and help someone in some small way if possible.

I decide to stop by Olivia Nelson's and check on her.

She looks surprised to see me when she opens the door. "Never expected to see you again," she says.

"Why's that?"

She looks like she hasn't slept or eaten in days, as if the stress and anxiety inside her are actually eating her alive.

"It's obvious, isn't it?" she says. "You think I'm nuts. You've given up on me."

I shake my head. "Neither of those things are true. I don't think you're crazy and haven't given up on you. I'm here because I want to help you. Please—"

"But you still think I'm making it all up."

"Prove me wrong," I say.

"How?"

"I heard you were refusing to submit to a psychological evaluation," I say.

"I know I'm not making it up."

"Then you have nothing to fear from the exam."

"Why are you really here again?" she asks.

"I told you. To check on you. See how you're doing."

"To see if I'm strangling or stabbing myself?"

Whether she's doing it to herself or someone else is doing it to her, she's still in danger and in need of serious help.

"No," I say. "Of course not. I'm just worried about you. I'd like to help you."

"I know you think you are, but you're not. You're not helping me. You're helping my stalker. You've got everyone convinced that he's not real, so now he'll be able to kill me."

"Let's say I'm wrong," I say. "What is the harm of being evaluated? Think about this . . . If I'm wrong . . . but you check into an inpatient facility for the evaluation anyway . . . you'll be safe from your stalker."

"I have nothing else to say to the man who signed my death warrant," she says, before stepping back and closing the door.

CHAPTER
EIGHTY-ONE

LATE THAT NIGHT as my family and much of the rest of the Northern Hemisphere are sleeping, I finish Carla's diary while attempting to keep my tears from landing on the pages.

I'm in my library-like study, a room that is among the most sacred places in the world to me, surrounded by books and art and mementos and photographs of my loved ones that include Carla and John Paul.

My deep grief turns to a fiery red rage when among the final pages I read the following:

I was drugged and raped last night.

I still can't believe it. I'm in shock.

I know who did it, but I can't tell anyone. Not only because most people wouldn't believe me and he and his family would make my life a living hell and try to take John Paul away from me, but I'm afraid of what John would do if he found out.

I feel so dirty and ashamed and used.

The thought of him touching me, being inside me, having complete and utter control over me to do whatever he wanted with me makes me so sick. I can't stop throwing up. I can't stop showering. I've scrubbed myself raw trying to wash him off me.

I always thought I was one of the lucky ones. So many of my friends were molested as children or raped in high school and college, but I never was.

I used to think the universe knew that not having a mother and having a drunk for a father was enough. But I was wrong.

How did this happen?

How did I let this happen?

How could I have been so stupid?

He's so gross. So disgusting. The thought of him. I can't. I've got to stop thinking about what he did to me.

I'm not hurt. He wasn't violent, but I was violated. He didn't brutalize me, at least physically, but mentally and emotionally he did.

I don't know what I'd do if it wasn't for John Paul. I can't do all the things I want to because I've got to be here for him.

I want to kill the bastard. I want to chop his dick off and shove it down his throat. I want to kill myself. But I can't do anything, and my precious boy is the reason why.

What else bad can happen to me? Surely this is it. I've reached my limit, right? No more bad shit for Carla, okay? I'm ready for more good things in my life like John Paul and John and Anna. No more bad. No more.

CHAPTER
EIGHTY-TWO

IT'S THE NEXT MORNING.

I haven't slept.

I'm not sleepy. I'm fueled up on fury, amped up on anger, filled with the desire to break something, to hurt someone. Not just anyone. A very particular someone.

It's Sunday morning. I'm still in my study.

Anna and the kids are visiting her parents in Dothan. Given the condition I'm in, I'm grateful for the time alone.

I keep going over and over it in my mind. Who could it be? Based on what she wrote, I don't think it was Mason or Easton. I don't think it was anyone she had ever dated or been involved with. So who?

I'm not sure how I'll be able to find out who it was. I just know I'm going to.

For now, I'm going to keep the information to myself, not make it part of the official investigation, not let anyone but Anna and Merrill know.

I have no way of knowing if whoever raped her also killed her, but chances are good that it's the same vile person.

I decide to return to the evidence, to re-examine everything as if for the first time.

As I read witness statements and listen to recordings of the interviews I think about the latest VSA results that indicated Easton and Meg were lying and Mason and Lily were telling the truth.

My phone vibrates in my pocket.

I pull it out and look at it. It's Michelle.

"Sorry to bother you on a Sunday," she says.

"Don't be," I say. "It's no bother."

"I heard back on the paternity tests," she says.

"Yeah?"

"Mason Hayes is not the father."

I start to say something but she continues.

"And neither is Easton."

I think about that.

"You there?" she says.

"Yeah. Just thinking."

"Any ideas who it might be?" she asks. "I thought for sure it'd be one of them."

I wonder if her rapist was the father and if he killed her or if the two crimes are unrelated.

"You thinking again?" she asks.

"Yeah, sorry."

"Well, if you want more to think about, the lab tech said to give her a call."

"Really?"

"Said she worked on a case with you in Atlanta more years ago than she cares to remember and would like to talk to you about something."

"Cool. Thanks."

"Let me know anything else I can do," she says. "I want this fucker caught."

CHAPTER
EIGHTY-THREE

"JOHN," Jodi Rambo says. "How the hell are you?"

"Been better," I say. "How are you, Jodi?"

"What's going on?" she asks.

I tell her.

"Oh, John, I'm so sorry. Doesn't surprise me at all that you're taking in strays or that you're working Carla's murder. Some things never change."

"How are things with you?" I ask.

"I'm good," she says. "Lots of blood under the bridge since I last saw you. Had a couple of kids. Had a couple of divorces. And helped put a lot of bad guys away. Couple of years back a new sheriff had me do some additional testing on the Atlanta Child Murders case, but . . . nothin' came of it. I just hate it that there's no justice for some of those poor kids. Hate that murderers have been walkin' around free all this time. People keep tellin' me we can't catch them all, and I say why. Why can't we?"

"I'm with you," I say. "I appreciate you."

"Well, you're about to appreciate me even more," she says.

"Oh yeah?"

"This is just between us," she says. "Off the record."

"Okay."

"The general paternity tests y'all had us run both came back negative," she says. "Neither suspect was the father. Those are essentially yes and no tests. Is the subject the father? Yes or no? But I noticed something on one of them that begged for a genetics test I wasn't asked or authorized to do."

"But you did it anyway?" I say.

"You know me," she says.

"Know and love," I say.

"For the paternity test we extract the mother's DNA and run the child's against the father's. When I did this for the Easton Stevens suspect, I noticed far more familial similarities that there should of been for him not to be the father. So I did a genetic test. A child gets half of his or her DNA from the father and half from the mother. Siblings typically share about twenty-five percent with each other. The fetus we tested here was male and he and Easton share all the same Y chromosomes and twenty-five percent of their DNA."

"Easton isn't the father," I say. "He's the brother."

"You didn't hear it from me," she says. "Just wanted you to know who to have tested next."

CHAPTER
EIGHTY-FOUR

HANK STEVENS RAPED CARLA.

No wonder he's been fighting so hard against our investigation. No wonder he told Easton to refuse to take the paternity test.

I realize with a sense of utter futility that even with Carla's journal entry and a paternity test we can never get a conviction for rape. All he has to say is that it was consensual. She doesn't name him in her diary but even if she had we still couldn't prosecute him—not for rape.

I think about what to do.

There's what I want to do and what I should do.

I want to kill him.

What I should do is keep working the case to see if he killed her and if I can build a case strong enough for a conviction.

What I decide to do is confront him and his family with this new revelation and see how they respond.

I will continue to work the case, continue to attempt to figure out who killed Carla, but for now I have to stand up for Carla, be her voice, her witness, against her rapist.

If tradition holds, Hank will be having Sunday lunch with

Easton and Meg—something he brags about never missing as part of his family values platform every time he runs for re-election.

CHAPTER EIGHTY-FIVE

"WE'RE HAVING LUNCH RIGHT NOW," Meg says. "Can you come back later. Or better yet . . . contact our attorney if you wish to speak to us."

I push past her and enter the house.

"Hey," she says. "Come back here. You can't—"

"What is it, Megan?" Hank says from the dining room.

I rush down the wide hallway beside the ornate staircase to find Hank and Easton sitting at the dining table, a large spread before them.

Meg walks in the room behind me. "I told him to go away. He just came in anyway."

"No need to be rude, Megan," Hank says. "John, would you join us for lunch? We'd be happy to have you."

As usual, Hank is wearing pressed khakis, a sky-blue Columbia fishing shirt, and brown work boots, though he doesn't do work that requires boots, and they always look like they were just taken out of the box.

Meg comes around in front of me and moves over behind her chair but doesn't sit.

"We got the paternity test results back," I say.

Easton looks confused, jerking his head from his wife to his father. "I didn't take a paternity test," he says.

I nod. "Yes, you did."

"No, I refused."

"We extracted your DNA from the envelope you licked."

"What? Why? You can't do that."

"Sure, we can. And we did. It's legal."

"We'll fight it," Hank says. "Nothing to worry about, son."

"Don't you want to know the results?" I ask Easton.

He shakes his head. "No."

"Why not? Is it because you and Meg have been lying to us?"

"We most certainly have not," Meg says.

"VSA says differently."

"I don't care if—"

"Easton," I say. "You're not the father."

They all looked relieved and let out a collective, audible sigh.

"Well, that's good news," Hank says. "See? I told y'all everything would be all right, didn't I?"

"You're not the father," I say, "because your father is. Your dad drugged and raped Carla. She was carrying your half-brother."

"*What*? No." He shakes his head violently as if the force will shake out the sounds and images inside.

"I will sue you for slander and defamation," Hank says. "You better not utter a word of this ever again."

I have been trying to avoid picturing Hank raping Carla, but with him in front of me now I am no longer able to keep the images at bay. The thought of his disgusting, fleshy, liquored-up old body on top of Carla makes me want to take a machete to him.

"Her diary says you raped her," I say. "And the genetic test says the boy she was carrying was yours."

"Daddy wouldn't do that," Easton says, sounding like a small child. "There's no way he would ever do anything like that to me."

I look at Meg, who has remained silent thus far.

Something is happening inside her. She appears to be weighing her options, deciding what to do.

"He tried it with me," she says.

"What?" Easton says. "No."

"Yes. He has hit on me so many times—sometimes right in front of you. Wake the fuck up. Be a man for once in your little life. He's tried to drug me too. He has a reputation, and you know it. All the young girls in town are told never to take a drink from him. They call him Hank Cosby."

"Stop it, Meg. No."

"Your own wife," she says. "And you're going to side with your rapist piece of shit dad? You're about to be a father yourself —unless he drugged and raped me without me knowing. I better get a paternity test too. But if our child is yours, what kind of father are you going to be? A weakling daddy's sugar boy who lies and cheats and defends a rapist?"

Easton shakes his head.

"Don't listen to her, son," Hank says.

"Now it's not just rumors and accusations," she says. "There's physical evidence. You can't keep on denying it. There's proof. He raped your girlfriend. He's tried to rape your wife. He's a sick fuck who—"

"If he fucked Carla," Easton says, "it's because she seduced him. She was a dirty slut and—"

I step over and slap him so hard on the face it knocks him out of the chair.

He stands up, holding his cheek, but doesn't make a move toward me.

"Do something," Meg says. "He just bitch slapped you, and you're just gonna take it."

"No, we're not," Hank says.

He's standing now, a small revolver in his hand pointed at me.

"Step away from my boy," Hank says. "He's right. It was

consensual. She begged me for it. She wanted to be with a rich and powerful man."

"You've got the drop on me," I say. "Think very carefully about your next move. You are pointing a weapon at a law enforcement officer. I'm about to withdraw my weapon and arrest you, so if you're going to shoot me now is the time. I'm not going to stop coming after you. I'm going to tell everyone what you did. I'm going to make the rest of your life absolute misery."

As he thumbs back the hammer of the revolver, Meg steps over in front of me.

"I'm a county commissioner," he says. "I own this town. You're a . . . You're not gonna come into my house and talk to me like this."

I withdraw my weapon.

"It's not your house," Meg says. "We're not your property." She turns toward Easton. "See? He thinks everything is his, your house, your wife, your—"

"He did help us with the down payment," Easton says.

I slide out from behind Meg, my weapon pointed at Hank. "Drop your weapon," I say.

Meg is shaking her head at her husband. "You're even more pathetic than I realized. I thought you just did what I told you, but . . . How can you be such a—"

"He's a good boy," Hank says. "He listens to me, which is more than I can say for you. Hopefully your boy will take after his daddy and not you."

There's something in the way he says it that leaves some doubt as to who he was referring to when he said *daddy*.

"Okay, John," Hank says, thumbing the hammer back down and placing the revolver on the table. "Don't shoot. You want to take me in? Fine. I'll be out in a matter of moments. You got nothin' on me. But boy do I have a lawsuit against you and the sheriff's office. I'm gonna break you and run your ass out of town. You just wait. You're about to—"

Meg springs forward and grabs the revolver from the table and points it at Hank.

"Say what you said earlier about my child's father," she says. "Who did you mean?"

"Meg," I say. "Put the gun down."

Though Meg is now the one with the gun, I keep my weapon pointed at Hank.

"Say it again," she says. "Tell me who the father of my child is. I want to know."

"Look, girly," he says. "It doesn't matter. It's the same either way. It's my DNA. Either way. He's my boy. Just like Easton is. And you're gonna learn your fuckin' place or you're gonna wind up like Easton's whore of a mama did."

Almost everything in me wants Meg to shoot Hank in the face. Almost. "Meg," I say. "Put the gun down. He's not going to get away with this."

"Yes, he will. He always does."

"Don't throw your life away for him. He's not worth it. Think about your baby."

"*My* baby?" she says. "It's not my baby. And never will be. He's right about that. There's no way I'm having this—"

Hank lunges toward her and grabs the gun.

She tries to shoot, but he takes it away from her.

"Drop it," I say.

He raises his hands. "I will," he says. "I just don't want to put it where she can grab it again."

His index finger is through the trigger guard, but he's not holding the gun with the rest of his hand and can't fire it from that position.

Meg falls to the floor crying.

Hank says, "I'm gonna toss the gun over toward you. Okay? Nice and slow. I'm just going to—"

Half of Hank's face is blown off as a booming explosion causes my ears to start ringing.

Meg screams and pounds her fists on the floor.

I turn to see Easton holding a shotgun.

"Drop it," I say, but I can't really hear myself say it.

He turns the weapon on himself and reaches down and feels around for the trigger.

"Don't do it," I say.

When he finally finds the trigger, he hesitates a moment.

"Easton," I say. "Don't do it. You can still have a life—a new life without being bullied and controlled all the time. Please."

His finger presses on the trigger but then eases up on it, and he throws the shotgun across the room.

He collapses to the floor and sits there in a heap as I call dispatch, and though Easton and Meg are only a few feet from each other, neither of them make a move toward the other.

CHAPTER
EIGHTY-SIX

"SO WHICH ONE of them killed Carla?" Arnie asks.

We are standing out in front of Easton and Meg's house as FDLE processes the crime scene.

I've already given a preliminary statement.

Meg and Easton are down at the sheriff's office giving their initial statements. Easton is in custody and will have first appearance in the morning.

"None of them," I say.

"*None of them*?" he asks.

"Easton used her. Meg threatened her. And Hank drugged and raped her. But none of them killed her."

"Are you sure?"

I realize I am—and that I hadn't been until this moment.

I nod. "Pretty sure."

My mind races through the evidence—the spontaneous, unplanned and unprepared nature of the crime. The strangulation and attempt to cover it up. The time we began looking for Carla and calling her friends. The fire at the McDaniel's cabin. The break-in of the storage box on the front porch of the Hayes's cabin. The use of the charcoal lighter fluid and the jumper cables. The disposal of Carla's vehicle and the seat being slid back.

Carla's body being carried up the embankment and hung on the tupelo branch. All of it.

I've known without knowing for a little while now—or my subconscious has known and my conscious mind has just caught up.

As I quickly think about the evidence, which doesn't take long because there's so little of it, I conclude there's probably not enough to get a conviction—even with the additional evidence of receipts and cell tower pings.

I decide to set a trap. And I'm self-aware enough to know that I'd want to even if there were a mountain of evidence. I crave confrontation more than conviction. I want to kill instead of arrest Carla's killer.

"Where are you going?" Arnie says.

As I race to my truck, I call Bailey Bozeman.

"You just can't get enough of me, can you?" she says. "Are the rumors true? Is Hank Stevens dead?"

"I'm sure all the rumors aren't true," I say, "but that one is."

"He kill Carla?"

"No, but he drugged and raped her."

"Killin' was too good for him."

"I need you to make a call for me. It's important. Maybe the most consequential call you'll ever make. Do it for me, and I'll buy your beer for the rest of your life."

"Tell me," she says.

"Call Mason Hayes. Act like you're a friend doin' him a favor, calling out of concern—or at least just wanting to be the first to tell him something you just overheard. Let him know that I'm coming to arrest him for Carla's murder after I pick up one more piece of evidence from the crime scene—one we overlooked until now. Will you do that?"

"Yeah, 'course. But if this helps you get the fuck for killin' Carla I'll buy *your* beer for the rest of your life."

CHAPTER
EIGHTY-SEVEN

"I DIDN'T KILL HER," Mason says.

I'm standing inside his family's cabin when he walks through the front door and makes his pronouncement.

"I know," I say.

I haven't been at the cabin long, just long enough to set up a hidden video camera and my phone to record what happens here.

"*You know?*" he says, confused. "Then why'd you—"

"I was bettin' on you telling your dad and him coming out here," I say.

"He—"

"He killed Carla," I say.

In the distance, the low echoey electrical rumble of thunder can be heard from the slow approach of a late-summer storm.

"What? No. He wasn't even in town."

"He came back early from his conference," I say. "He just came back even earlier than anyone knew." I say it as if I know it for a fact instead of it being part of a deduction. "When we couldn't get you or Carla, we called your parents. Your dad was one of the first people I spoke to. I'm sure he talked to you too. As usual, his first response was to help clean up behind you.

Gainesville is only three hours away. He came back then. Witnesses down there and up here will confirm it, but we don't need them to. The towers his cell pinged against will tell the tale.

"I don't think he came to kill her. Still not sure why he did, but that's what he did. He choked the life out of her, then staged the ridiculous hanging with the jumper cables from the locked storage box on the front porch. That's how we know it was not premeditated, wasn't planned. But one of many mistakes he made was the way he staged the break-in of the box. He used his key to unlock the lock—because he couldn't cut it. He didn't have bolt cutters or anything. Then he threw the lock into the swamp. We found it undamaged. Then he kicked the hasp and splintered the wood so it hung down. But the lock should've still been in the hasp. If he didn't have a key, if it wasn't him, the lock should've still been locked on the hasp—and the hasp should've been broken off either the lid or the side. Then he used the charcoal lighter fluid to burn his and Carla's clothes at the McDaniel's place.

"Even burned, his rubber boots would match the prints we found here and across the river at the site of the hanging. Where does he keep his rubber boots? In his boat? At the house? I guarantee they are gone. And either there are none or he has a new pair and we'll be able to track their recent purchase. The fire got away from him. When I saw him the next day, his face was glowing red and his voice was raspy. I thought it was from too much time by the pool or high blood pressure and singing Karaoke at his conference, but it was from being too close to the fire and smoke inhalation and from yelling for Carla when he came out here. And then there's the—"

I stop speaking as the barrel of a handgun is pressed to the back of my head.

"That's enough," Will Hayes says.

I raise my hands though he didn't tell me to. Glancing back at him, I see that even now in these dire circumstances he is in green scrubs and crocs.

In the momentary silence I can hear more thunder rolling around, but the storm is still a good distance away.

"*Dad?*" Mason says. "You . . . Is he . . . right? You killed Carla?"

"I didn't mean to," he says. "Didn't intend to. Was just trying to get her to calm down. She was . . . She was very upset. She couldn't believe you left her. Tell the truth, I couldn't believe that either. She was making all sorts of accusations, sayin' I had drugged and raped her and . . . She said she was going to bring the family down. Do you have any idea how hard I've worked to have what we have. A chubby kid everyone dismissed or ignored. I worked my ass off and for a long, long time. I became a doctor. A fuckin' doctor. I scored your mom. She didn't even look at me in high school. Built a successful practice and a lifestyle my parents could've never dreamed of.

"I couldn't let her take all that away. I couldn't. And not just for me but for you and your mom and all those who count on me. She was . . . She was a sad, pathetic . . . She wasn't like us. She wasn't . . . I wasn't about to let her steal what is ours. But I didn't mean to kill her. I didn't. I swear. I just . . . I was trying to get her under control. That's all. I guess I didn't realize how hard or how long I was . . . I didn't mean any of this." His voice changes and lowers a little and to me he says, "What's the other evidence that was overlooked?"

"It was over there under the bed," I say. "But I already—"

He doesn't know what he's doing. He's holding the gun high on my head and is way too close to me. As his attention is on the made up evidence, I make my move.

Leaning my head into the gun, I spin around, bringing my left elbow up under his gun arm, pushing the gun away from my head. I then hook my arm around his and break his elbow down, wrenching his shoulder around and causing his rotator cuff to rotate more than it was made to. I then bring my right hand up, grab my left hand, and pull up even harder.

He screams in pain as his shoulder wrenches around even farther than it was made to.

As he drops the gun, I use the heel of my right hand to break his nose and knock him down.

As he falls to the ground, he's just a few feet from his gun.

Standing over him, I neither make a move for his gun nor withdraw my own.

I glance at his gun trying to draw his attention to it.

He tries to reach for it, but his dislocated shoulder won't let him.

I step over and kick it over to him.

He looks up at me. The confusion on his face morphing into fear.

The crackling thunder is closer now, louder, but not close enough for lightning or rain.

"You . . . You set all this up," he says. "You brought me here to . . . what? Kill me?"

"You killed Carla to protect all you worked so hard for," I say. "Do the same now. I'm about to take everything from you. Protect it. Stop me from taking what's yours."

He shakes his head and begins to cry.

"Grab the gun," I yell. "Now."

"No. I . . . I can't. You'll kill me."

"I'm gonna kill you either way. This is your only chance to stop me."

"I'm not a killer," he says. "I was just tryin' to protect my son. I did it for him."

"Then I'll kill him and let you live with that."

"You're willin' to kill," he says. "For Carla. That's all I was doin'. Protecting my boy. It's no different."

He killed Carla to protect himself as much as his son, but I get what he' saying, and though it is different, it's similar enough to give me pause.

"Pick up that weapon," I say. "Protect your son. Protect yourself."

He shakes his head. "I . . . can't."

He begins to cry even harder.

He's weak and pathetic, and almost more than anything in this world I want to press the barrel of my .9mm to the eleven of his furrowed brow between his eyes and squeeze the trigger.

Almost.

The only thing I want to do more than that is go home to my family and hold Carla's son, now my son, and let him know he is safe and loved, and I can't do that if I kill his mother's killer in cold blood.

"If I let you and your boy live, will you give a full confession?"

He nods. "I will. I swear."

And though I know he'll try to weasel out of it later, maybe the video from today along with all the other evidence will be enough for a conviction. Right now all I can do is hope that it is because I can't kill him. I thought I could. I wanted to. But I can't. In a way I feel like I'm failing Carla again, and maybe I am, but I'm not failing her son, and I have to believe that's what she'd want more than for me to kill her killer.

CHAPTER
EIGHTY-EIGHT

THAT NIGHT I hold John Paul close to me for as often and as long as he will allow.

As we have family dinner and play games together and walk up town for Birdie's Brew coffee for me and Anna and Shoobie's ice cream for the kids, I am continuously hugging and holding him, and when he's had enough I do the same with Anna and the other children.

Even as I am checking on and loving on the kids, Anna is checking on and loving on me.

Later that night we all fall sleep reading books to the kids in our bed.

At some point, Anna wakes me up, and we ease out of the bed, leaving the kids sleeping there.

I follow her through the house and out the backdoor to our patio, where we sit beneath a sky full of stars and a big, bright half-moon in the first hints of fall.

The storm is long gone, and the night is coolish and quiet, a gentle breeze rustling the branches and leaves of the trees around the lake.

Eventually, I tell her what I need to.

"I'm so glad you couldn't kill him," she says.

"I had every intention of doing it," I say.

"If you had . . . you might not be here with me right now. You might have missed all our family time tonight—all of our family time for a long time to come. And that is unimaginable to even think about."

"That's what kept me from doing it," I say.

"Don't get me wrong," she says. "I wish he was in the morgue right beside Hank Stevens where they both belong, but not for the price we'd have to pay for him to be there."

I take her hand in mine.

"Anything that takes me away from you and the kids is too high a price to pay."

We sit in silence holding each other's hand for a long moment after that, the truth of it permeating the atmosphere around us.

"I feel so bad for all that Carla is going to miss," she says. "And not just of John Paul's life, but for what could have been her own."

"It's hard to reconcile how incredibly good and sweet this life is for some and how unbelievably painful and tragic it is for others."

She nods. "It certainly is."

We sit with that for a few moments.

Eventually, she says, "So grateful for our dads. Can't help but believe none of this would've ever happened if Rudy, Hank, and Will had been better men and fathers."

I start to say something, but she says, "I'm so glad our girls have you. So glad Nash and John Paul now have you too."

She pauses for a moment and again I start to say something, but she continues.

"Wonder what kind of father Olivia Nelson had or has," she says.

"We'll probably find out before it's over," I say.

"How sure are you that what's happening to her is self-inflicted?"

"Pretty sure," I say "but we're gonna find that out before it's over too."

"So much suffering in the world," she says.

"Too much," I say.

"We alleviate some of it," she says.

"Some," I say.

"You more than me," she adds. "You more than most."

"Not enough."

"It's enough," she says. "Enough for Nash. Enough for John Paul. Enough for all the families of the victims you've brought justice to over the years. All the would-be victims you saved by catching all the killers and robbers and rapists and putting them away."

"Nothing feels like enough right now," I say.

"I know. And in these moments you have to trust me and believe me when I tell you it's enough. You're enough. We're enough. Our family is enough. What you do is enough."

And though I don't believe it and can't fathom it, I choose to trust her, to believe her, and for now that is enough.

ALSO BY MICHAEL LISTER

Blue Blood

And the Sea Became Blood

The Blood-Dimmed Tide

Blood and Sand

A John Jordan Christmas

Blood Lure

Blood Pathogen

Beneath a Blood-Red Sky

Out for Blood

What Child is This?

Blood Reckoning

(Burke and Blade Mystery Thrillers)

The Night Of

The Night in Question

All Night Long

(Jimmy Riley Novels)

The Girl Who Said Goodbye

The Girl in the Grave

The Girl at the End of the Long Dark Night

The Girl Who Cried Blood Tears

The Girl Who Blew Up the World

(Merrick McKnight / Reggie Summers Novels)

Thunder Beach

A Certain Retribution

Blood Oath

Blood Shot

(Remington James Novels)

Double Exposure

(includes intro by Michael Connelly)

Separation Anxiety

Blood Shot

(Sam Michaels / Daniel Davis Novels)

Burnt Offerings

Blood Oath

Cold Blood

Blood Shot

(Love Stories)

Carrie's Gift

(Short Story Collections)

North Florida Noir

Florida Heat Wave

Delta Blues

Another Quiet Night in Desperation

(The Meaning Series)

Meaning Every Moment

The Meaning of Life in Movies

Sign up for Michael's newsletter by clicking here or go to
www.MichaelLister.com and receive a free book.

Ingram Content Group UK Ltd.
Milton Keynes UK
UKHW012333240723
425713UK00014B/260/J

9 781947 606920